RHINELAND INHERITANCE

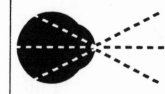 This Large Print Book carries the
Seal of Approval of N.A.V.H.

RHINELAND INHERITANCE

T. Davis Bunn

G.K. Hall & Co.
Thorndike, Maine

Published in 1995 by arrangement with
Bethany House Publishers.

This story is entirely a creation of the author's imagination.
No parallel between any persons, living or dead, is intended.

G.K. Hall Inspirational Collection.

Set in 16 pt. News Plantin by Rick Gundberg.

Printed in the United States on permanent paper.

Library of Congress Catalog Card Number: 95-077171

This book is dedicated to
Gil Morris
For the friendship
And the challenge.

Prologue

The Former Third Reich of National
Socialist Germany
October 1945

Jake knew something big was in the air the moment he closed the door in his fiancee's face.

Maybe he knew before. Maybe that was what gave him the strength to leave her photograph taped to the back of his locker. Six months had passed since she had written about her new lover. Yet the tattered photo had remained with him through two more postings and the end of the war. But no more.

Captain Jake Burnes set his cap at the proper angle, hefted his worldly belongings, and marched out to meet his future.

The future stood waiting for him in the form of a new-old buddy, Captain Sam Marshall, head of the local MP garrison. The war had taught both men the trick of making friends fast, then losing them even faster.

"Need a hand?"

"Thanks, I can manage," Jake replied. "I decided to lighten the load."

"Come again?"

"Never mind." Jake started off toward the camp's main gate. To his left sprawled one of the Allies' internment camps, full to overflowing both with former German soldiers and the never-ending stream of refugees.

Marshall swung in beside him, matching Jake's stride with the unconscious habit borne on a thousand parade grounds. "Got a jeep waiting for you up at the gate."

Jake hid his gratitude behind pretended surprise. "This the normal treatment for somebody who's just been kicked off base?"

"Just thought a buddy might need a lift, is all," Marshall replied. "And maybe a little escort duty."

"You what?"

"You've made some enemies around here," Marshall said.

Jake's shoulders bounced once in a humorless laugh. "Tell me something I don't already know."

They walked on in silence for a time before Marshall said, "Got my marching orders this morning. Along with all my men."

That stopped him. "Connors can't be meaning to send all of you home at once."

"That's where you're wrong," Marshall replied. "The good colonel's decided to get rid of all my men. And me. Next week."

"He plans to guard the camp with those untrained gorillas of his?" Jake glanced over the fence to where one of the newly arrived MPs walked in bored guard duty. The man was built like a full-grown bull, all shoulders and swagger.

"That's what it looks like." Marshall's eyes followed Jake's. "Another dozen piled in this morning. Drawn from every division in Europe, by the sounds of it. None of them ever pulled MP duty in their lives. Only time they ever saw a stockade was when they were inside."

Jake shook his head. "Doesn't make sense, sending his only experienced men home all at once like that."

"There's a lot around here that doesn't make any sense," Marshall replied. "And more every day."

"Such as?"

"Heard some of them talking last night, filling in the new boys. Work details, from the sounds of it. Nothing to do with any guard duty I've ever heard of." Marshall watched the sentry make another pass. "Sounded like a bunch of bandits making ready for the big heist."

"Then you must have heard wrong," Jake said flatly. "That whole camp doesn't have two plug nickels to rub together."

"Maybe," Marshall said doubtfully. "They kept saying something about orders direct from Colonel Connors. Strange to see a commanding officer take such interest in new MPs."

Jake resumed walking. "Yeah, well, if I don't ever hear that name again, it'll be too soon."

"They were talking about you, too," Marshall went on. "What I heard made me think you might stay healthier if I were to see you off base."

"Why would they bother with me?" Jake returned the sentry officer's laconic salute. "I'm history."

"Ever wonder why Connors would be so eager to get rid of his best officer? Not to mention the only man on his staff who speaks passable German."

Jake hefted his duffle bag into the back of the jeep. "Maybe he's got somebody else in mind for the job."

"Seems like a lot of trouble to go through over a grudge," Marshall persisted.

"I gave up trying to figure the colonel out a long time ago." Jake started to climb in; then something made him hesitate. He turned back around, and spotted a young kid watching through the wires.

The boy was no more than twelve or thirteen, but nonetheless wore the ragged remnants of a uniform. They had come across a lot of such child-warriors in the war's last days. In his frantic final effort, Hitler had sent out whole battalions of the very young and very old. Most had received no training whatsoever. Many had not even been armed.

Jake saw a pair of dark eyes stare at him with the fathomless depths of one without hope. He had seen too many young eyes carry such expressions as he had trudged and fought his way through the war. Still, the gaze tugged at his heart. It always did.

For some reason he could not explain, Jake lifted his hand in farewell.

The boy remained still as stone for a time, then suddenly thrust both arms out through the wire. Fingers clawed the air, reaching for Jake, begging for what he could not give. The boy's face became a mask of soundless pleading.

"Hey!" An MP with the battered face of a long-time boxer lumbered over. "Back behind the wire!"

Long before the MP reached him, the boy spun and fled into the camp.

Jake stood and watched the vacant space where the boy had been, and wondered why after two years of active duty he still could not stop hurting for the kids. He shrugged it away as best he could, climbed into the jeep, and said, "Let's go."

Chapter One

To Jake, this new colonel seemed a good joe —
at least, as far as any superior officer could be.
"Captain Jake Burnes, right?"

"Yessir, reporting for duty."

"Take a load off, Captain." Colonel Beecham
buried his nose back in Jake's file. "Let's see.
Left Officer Training School in October '42, got
to the front just in time for the push up through
Italy. In the meantime you've earned yourself a
silver star, a bronze star, a purple heart, and a
string of medals from here to Okinawa. What'd
you do, son, decide it was your own private war?"

"Never much liked sitting around, sir."

"No, it doesn't sound like it." He flipped over
another page. "Don't see any mention of you
speaking French."

"Not a word, sir."

"So they assigned you as liaison for incoming
French troops." The colonel snorted. "Another
example of army logic."

"Temporary liaison, sir," Jake corrected.

"That so?" Colonel Beecham searched the file.
"When are you due for release, Captain?"

"Seven weeks, sir. Just before Christmas."

The colonel squinted down an invisible rifle barrel at Burnes. "They assigned me a liaison officer who doesn't know a word of French and is going home in seven weeks?"

"Looks that way, sir."

"Whose feathers did you ruffle, Captain? General Eisenhower's?"

"Nossir. Only Colonel Connors', sir."

"Only." A glimmer of humor appeared in the steely gaze. "That must be Cut-Throat Connors, isn't that what they call him?"

"I wouldn't know, sir."

"I hear he'd sell his soul and mortgage his own mother for a star on his shoulder. What'd you do, son?"

"Nothing really, sir. Just a difference of opinion."

"Come on, Captain. Cut to the chase. Sure as gunfire in a battle zone, there's not a friend of Connors in sight. Let's hear it."

Jake decided the colonel really meant it. "I was responsible for a section of the Oberkirch internment camp."

"I know that. So?"

"Just before I arrived they'd had a couple of suicides among the former German soldiers. The officer whose place I took spoke some German and managed to get some of the men to talk with him. Seems like they'd been growing despondent over what was waiting for them outside — cities pretty much destroyed, no food, less

13

work, chaos everywhere. The officer started looking around for some way to improve morale, and decided to train a couple of squads in touch football." Jake shrugged. "Since I speak German, he asked me to take over where he left off."

"Connors is awful proud of his football team, isn't he."

"Yessir."

Colonel Connors was responsible for security in the region north of Offenburg. It was well known that he was constantly scouting for football material, and any enlisted man who made his team won an MP billet and an extra stripe.

"What'd he do, challenge your German boys to a game? Put a couple of side bets down?"

"More than a couple," Burnes replied. "From what I heard, sir."

"And then your boys went out and whupped his pride and joy." The smile finally surfaced. "Wish I'd been there to see that."

"It was some game, sir," Burnes said with evident satisfaction.

"Worth getting stuck with a bunch of foreigners for your last posting?"

Burnes shrugged. "Can't be worse than guarding ten thousand defeated German soldiers."

Colonel Beecham settled back in his chair. "So you speak some German. How much is some?"

"I guess I can get around pretty well, sir. I was studying it before I got called up."

"Maybe you'll be of some use, after all. I've got quite a few bilinguals in French and English,

14

but almost no German speakers. Just a chaplain who's almost never here and a young lady who's already too busy by half. Any chance of you changing your mind, maybe signing on for another tour?"

"None at all," Jake replied flatly. "Sir."

"It's like that, is it? You got somebody waiting for you back home?"

"Not anymore," Jake replied bitterly.

"She dear-johned you?"

"Six months ago, sir." The letter had simply said, don't come back expecting to find things like they used to be, because what used to be isn't there anymore. "Guess she got tired of waiting."

"Family?"

"Not anymore," Jake repeated, more softly this time.

The colonel's leathery features creased with concern. "While you were over here?"

Jake nodded. "Both at once. They had an automobile accident."

The letter had been waiting for him when his platoon had marched into Rome. The fact that he hadn't slept for three days had partly numbed the pain. The letter had been written by their elderly next-door neighbor and family friend. Snowstorm. Icy road. Oncoming truck. His dad had not made it to the hospital. His mother had died two days later in her sleep. No apparent injuries, the doctors couldn't explain it. Jake was sad but not sorry. His mother would have been lost without his father around.

"Tough," the colonel said, and clearly meant it. "What about brothers or sisters?"

"One brother," Jake said, telling the rest in a weary voice. "He was leading a mortar squad on D-Day. They were coming off the boat ramp onto the beach at Normandy. A German '88 round hit the ramp and took out the whole squad."

The colonel said softly, "I lost a son on the beaches."

Both men gazed at a spot somewhere between them for a moment of pained and silent remembering. The colonel was the first to speak again. "Sounds as if the only family you've got left is the army."

If you could call a group that had tried its level best to get him killed for two solid years a family. "Guess that's about it, sir."

"Well, we'll see if we can't bring you around to our way of thinking. We've got seven weeks to soften you up." Colonel Beecham leaned back and hefted a pair of size thirteens onto the corner of his desk. "Am I to assume that Colonel Connors did a thorough job of briefing you on your new responsibilities?"

"All I know," Jake replied, "is that right now I'm sitting in a squad room in what I hope is Badenburg. Sir."

"Okay, here's the scoop. As you may know, the Allies are in the process of splitting Germany into four sections, each to be governed by a different occupying force. France has been given responsibility for two portions extending out from their border. One of the sections is right here, the other is up on the other side of Karlsruhe.

"For the past few months, the French have been too busy taking care of business at home to worry much about this region, so we've been holding the fort for them. Sort of, anyway. Temporary measures tend not to hold too well in the army. But that's almost over now. The French are due in here the week after Christmas. The only American base that will remain in this area is Karlsruhe, which is where we are planning to consolidate. There and Stuttgart and Pforzheim, which remain in the American zone. Are you with me?"

"So far, yessir."

"Right." Without turning around, Beecham pointed toward the map on the wall behind him. "That red line you see there is the border between France and Germany. That's our responsibility. The place is like a sieve right now. We've got upwards of a thousand refugees pouring through there every night. I don't know where they're hoping to go, 'cause the French sure don't want them. Now that it's getting cold, the morning patrols are coming across bodies. It's a bad business, Captain. We didn't fight this dang war to have civilians dying in the bushes. Not in my area. The way I see it, we've got a responsibility to these people. If the war's over, then it's over, and we've got to start treating them like the human beings they are. Have you

17

got any problems with that?"

"None at all, sir."

"Okay. Now, I've got seventeen hundred men under my command right now, but like all these places around here, we're losing them fast. The border area isn't as high up on the brass's list of priorities as I think it should be. As far as they're concerned, if these Eastern European refugees want to keep running until they drop, that's their business. But not for me. Nossir. They need to be properly cared for in the camps until we can get some kind of permanent billet sorted out. Am I getting through?"

"Loud and clear, sir."

"As I said, there's an American contingent up here at Karlsruhe. They're supposed to be helping out, at least until the French are settled in and up to snuff. But they're so tied up trying to find space for all the incoming personnel and equipment, they're busier than a one-legged man in a polka contest."

The colonel pointed a finger the size of a large-caliber gun barrel directly at Jake's chest. "That's your job, son. I want a concerted effort by all the military in this region, both those here now and those coming in, to help us close that border. Think you can do that?"

"I'll sure give it a try, sir."

"Good man. Our responsibility runs all the way from Karlsruhe right down to the Swiss border below Mulhouse. Almost exactly one hundred miles, a lot of which is heavily forested. What isn't covered in woodland, well, this war has made to look like something dragged up from hell."

"A tough job," Burnes said.

"An impossible job, with the men I've got right now," Beecham corrected. "Which means it is positively vital that you get the other forces to help us out."

"From the sound of your voice I guess they're not all that interested."

"Some are, some aren't. Some of our commanders are still too busy fighting an enemy that has already surrendered to worry about civilian casualties. Others just don't care."

"There are men like that in every army, sir."

"Tell me about it," Beecham agreed wearily. "So your job, Captain, is to make them care."

"Yessir," Burnes said, rising to his feet.

"One more thing." The colonel's tone turned cold. "You're going to hear about it soon enough, so I might as well be the one to tell you. There's a lot of scuttlebutt going around just now about Nazi treasure. You know the SS used Badenburg as a sort of private resort."

"I've heard the same stories as everybody else, sir."

"So you've probably heard the tales about them burying everything from the Mongol diamond to Cleopatra's throne in the hills around here." The colonel rose to his feet. "I'm not going to waste my breath by ordering you not to go treasure hunting, Captain. But if I ever find out you've been in derelict of duty because of some fairy

19

tale about the lost kingdom of Nod, or hear you've been out gallivanting on army time, I'll personally have your hide. You reading me, Captain?"

"Loud and clear, sir."

"You'll be working with a Captain Servais, who used to be with the Fighting Free French. Good man. Served with the Americans for a time. Highly decorated. You two should get along fine."

"I'm sure we will, sir."

"I've got a woman on my staff who was seconded from the new government staffers arriving in Berlin. Her name is Anders — Sally Anders. They sent her here to act as liaison with the incoming French forces. Quite a dynamo. She's off somewhere in the city just now, but any paperwork you need doing or red tape that gets in your way, she's your gal."

"I'll give it my best shot, sir."

"That's what I like to hear." The colonel's attention was already caught by something else on his desk. "Have Sergeant Morrows show you to your billet. Dismissed."

The colonel's office was in staff headquarters, which was situated in what appeared to be the only intact building on the road leading to town. It had formerly been a large manor house, and its ornate brick and iron fencing was now topped off with military-issue barbed wire. The great iron gates had been replaced by a guardhouse and standard checkpoint crossbar. The large formal grounds were now sectioned off into smaller

20

self-contained units for stores, motor pool, staff quarters, infirmary, and parade ground.

The main base was a mile farther up the road running away from town, and had clearly been designed for a much larger contingent than the one which now occupied it. The camp was built on a hill overlooking the ruins of Badenburg. The ground had been cleared from the dense forest that surrounded them on all sides. Fresh-cut tree stumps, some of them as broad as six feet across, jutted from the snow-covered ground between the huts. Rutted tracks frozen to iron hardness ran in long straight army lines between the rows of billets. The Quonsets lumped across the hilltop like rows of metal measles.

Sergeant Morrows drove Jake across the frozen, rutted ground. He stopped before a Quonset, distinct from its neighbors only by the number painted on its side. Beecham's aide was a heavy-set sergeant who slid and cursed his way over the icy earth toward the entrance. "It ain't supposed to turn this cold for another three months, so they say. Guess we're in for one hard winter. You ever seen anything like this freeze, Captain?"

"I came up via Italy," Jake replied. "Never had much time for cold weather."

"Italy, huh. Fought with Patton?"

"So they say."

"Yeah, I never had much time for the high brass myself." Morrow's grin exposed a great expanse of yellow. "You liberate many of those

21

signorinas yourself, Captain?"

Burnes shook his head. The colonel's aide was a man to keep as an ally. If possible. "The stories never tell you about how all the signorinas have fathers," Jake replied. "Or how all the fathers have shotguns."

"Yeah? Well, you won't have that trouble around here." The sergeant leered and shouldered the door open. "This is your billet, Captain. The whole barracks for the two of you. And look who's here. Captain Servais, this is your new teammate, Captain Burnes, late of Patton's army."

The man rolled from his bunk in the fluid motion of one accustomed to coming instantly awake. The man walked forward with the cautious gaze of someone who had learned in life-and-death struggles to measure all partners with great care. "Captain Burnes, did I hear that correctly?"

"You speak English," Jake said, accepting the man's ironhard grip. "You don't know what a relief that is."

"Captain Burnes here don't have no French, but he speaks the local Kraut lingo," Morrows drawled. "Well, I'll leave you gents to get acquainted. Anything you need, Captain, and all that." Morrows turned and stomped away.

Jake watched Morrows' broad back retreating. When the door closed, he turned to find Servais watching him with a knowing gaze. "Sergeant Morrows has the ability to find anything, anywhere, anytime."

"I figured the colonel wasn't keeping him

around for his charm," Jake said.

"Put the sergeant down in the middle of Antarctica, and in thirty minutes he'd have enough gear to equip an entire platoon," Servais said, motioning toward the hut's murky depths. "Will you take coffee? I don't have anything stronger, I'm afraid."

"Coffee's fine," Burnes replied, following Servais between bunks of rusted springs and rolled-up mattresses. "I can't get over how well you speak English. You sound almost American."

"I spent my summers as a waiter serving tourists on the French Riviera, starting when I was twelve," Servais explained, placing a battered pot on a small gas burner. "I soon discovered that the English gave better tips if I could speak to them. Then during the war I spent some time with American troops."

"Free French?" Burnes asked, dropping his gear beside a bunk.

Servais nodded. He filled a mug with coffee and handed it over. "Condensed milk there on the table beside you."

"Thanks." Burnes poured in some milk and took a noisy sip. "I heard some good things about the FFF. Never had a chance to see for myself."

"Where did you serve?"

"Italy, mostly," Burnes replied. "I walked every road from Salerno to Milan, or so it felt at the time. How about you?"

"North Africa, then here." Servais glanced at the medals decorating Jake's uniform. "I take it

23

the pretty ribbons were not earned from the back-seat of a command jeep."

"Not all of them, anyway." Jake motioned toward a dress jacket hanging from a nail in the wall, its array of medals glimmering in the glare of the single overhead bulb. "Looks like you carry your own set of stories."

Servais had the sort of strong, ugly face that many women would find irresistible — all jutting angles and craggy folds. His nose was a great lump jutting above a full mouth, his eyes black and piercing. He was not a big man, standing well short of six feet and slender to the point of appearing permanently hungry. But he carried himself with the solid assurance of one well used to his own strength. "What do you call yourself?"

"Jake. What about you?"

"Pierre." Servais glanced at his watch. "I'm scheduled for a patrol. But first I have to go by and pick up orders at HQ. You could change into fatigues and join me, if you like."

As with most army jeeps, the canvas top had long since worn out, there was no heat, and the exhaust puffed through holes in the flooring, nearly choking them every time Servais slowed down. Which he seldom did.

"I'm splitting my men up so the ones with field experience outnumber the newcomers two to one," Pierre shouted over the whining motor. "I don't know how long that will last, if they keep sending in new recruits as fast as they are now."

As far as Burnes could see, the only good thing about Pierre's driving was that he hit the bumps so hard it lifted Jake's backside off the seat and kept him from freezing solid to the cracked leather padding. "You survived the war just to die now?" Jake asked, keeping a white-knuckled grip on the jeep's rattling frame.

"A lot of my soldiers are just barely eighteen," Pierre went on. "They come from the newly liberated provinces, and they want to show their patriotism by acting tough toward the defeated Germans. I need the soldiers who actually experienced the war to keep them in line. The problem is, my best men are leaving. Their time is up and they're being discharged. Either that, or they are being rounded up and sent to Indochina. I don't know how I'm going to be able to handle the new ones without them."

The jeep did a four-wheel skid around an icy corner, almost wrapped itself around a tree, caught hold of the road at the last possible moment, and barreled on. Burnes shouted, "It's amazing you ever survived to fight the Germans."

Pierre slowed marginally. "These new soldiers are just kids. Full of anger and spite. Some of them feel like cowards because they weren't old enough to prove themselves. Most claim to have been in the underground. Some probably were. All of them are dangerous. To themselves and the Germans."

Staff Headquarters, and Colonel Beecham's office, was located in one of the few intact houses

25

on the southwestern side of Badenburg. After turning in his duty rosters, Pierre took the time to show Burnes around. The officers' mess was located in what had probably once been a grand ballroom, although the chandelier had long since been dislodged by a bomb. A few links from the heavy chain still dangled from the ceiling. Directly underneath, the shattered flooring had been hastily relaid with stone. It was hard to find wood these days, as the locals were stealing anything they could find to warm their homes.

Jake was still looking at the ornamental frieze encircling the ceiling when they rounded the corner, which was why he walked directly into one of the most beautiful women he had seen in two long years. She backed up a step, set her cap in place, said, "You're straightforward, soldier. I'll have to give you that."

Jake stammered up an, "I'm sorry, ma'am. I didn't —"

"Apologies accepted. I wasn't looking either." She was lithe and tall, with auburn hair piled and pinned beneath the cap. Her eyes were the color of smoke from a winter's fire. "Are you supposed to be shepherding this poor lost lamb around, Pierre?"

"Captain Burnes is quite capable of looking after himself," Pierre replied. "How are you, Sally?"

"Busy. You'll have to excuse me." She stepped between them. "Nice to have met you, Captain, I suppose."

The two men watched Sally as she walked down

the corridor and out of sight. Jake realized he had been holding his breath. He straightened and asked, "Who was that *that?*"

"Sally Anders." Pierre's eyes had not shifted from the point where Sally had disappeared from view. "Also known as the Ice Queen. Late of Ottowa. Secretary to the general staff."

"Married?"

"Her fiance was lost at sea. North Atlantic convoy duty." Pierre shook his head. "My friend, if I'd had someone like that waiting for me at home, I would have learned to walk on water."

The three platoons were drawn up under a gray sky that threatened to blanket them with yet more snow. Pierre's orders were given from the hood of the jeep. Jake Burnes understood not a word. Yet his lack of French could not keep him from observing the casual hold which Pierre maintained over the power of command. The troops listened carefully to his clipped sentences. He lightened them with a joke that brought smiles to most faces. He gathered them together and made them feel a part of something larger. Jake did not need to know the words to understand what was happening. He was watching a leader.

Pierre jumped from the jeep, said in English, "There's been a lot of movement down the southern stretch. I thought I'd take them myself today. Care to come along?"

Jake understood that he was being tested. He knew that it would jeopardize their work together if he pointed out that this excursion was not part of his duty roster. "Whatever you say."

Pierre placed a grizzled Belgian sergeant-major on point and two hard-eyed corporals as back sentries, and ordered them to move out. They were soon tramping along paths that were invisible under their mantle of snow, trusting their sergeant's experience to take them out and bring them back.

The pace was hard. The ground was broken, with invisible traps for the unwary beneath the white covering. They moved in a silence disturbed only by grunts and heavy breathing.

Every mile or so they would come upon a guardpost, usually invisible until they were almost upon it, any roughness from the recent construction hidden under winter's blanket. A half-frozen man would crawl down from his tree house, stamp up and down, slapping feeling back into his body, and make a shivering report. A new man would be assigned to shinny up the tree ladder. Once in place, the squad would be again under way.

They had been going long enough for Jake to work up a fair lather when the ground exploded at his feet. This time there was no bomb; only a young deer that had taken shelter in a steep-sided levee. The deer bounded upward, throwing up a glorious blast of snow, then disappeared into the woods.

Jake leaned against a tree, slowing his breath and letting the weakness drain from his legs. Around him the men laughed with relief. Jake smiled at chatter he did not hear, and recalled his last injury, when a land mine had exploded less than a dozen feet away. The point man had hit the trip wire, and had simply vanished. Jake had caught a sliver of shrapnel across his forehead, slicing him open clean to the bone. There had been more blood than damage, and after a couple dozen stitches and one night in the mobile infirmary, Jake had been sent back to his squad.

As he stood and gathered himself, Jake glimpsed something moving rapidly to one side of his field of vision.

"There!" he shouted, then was up and after the running figure.

The man raced through the trees in great leaps that lifted him clear of the clinging snow. Jake felt the air pumping in and out of his lungs as he pounded after him. The man was carrying a dark sack, that much Jake could see in his fleeting glimpses as he chased him through the woods. Twice the sack caught in low branches, each time granting Jake a breath's span to close the gap. Behind him he heard whistles and shouts and crashing sounds, but he had no time to look around. No time for anything but the challenge of the chase.

Then the shot blazed out and smacked the tree beside him, throwing a cloud of snow into his eyes. Jake's war-trained reactions reasserted themselves. He was down and rolling, then crouched and searching, pistol in hand without knowing how it had come free from the holster.

Pierre crawled up beside him, breathless. "Did you see where the shot came from?"

Jake made a vague gesture forward and to the right. "Somewhere up there."

Pierre motioned for two soldiers to head over, the others to fan out. Then forward. Careful, now. Cautious. But as fast as possible.

They caught the man's tracks and followed them until it began to snow. Dusk was gathering, the men were cold, the quarry had vanished. Somewhere up ahead, the Rhine River marked the border with France, but without proper night gear they would find it by falling in.

Pierre was preparing to turn them around. But Jake wanted to press on. Had to. Someone had shot at him. Wasn't the war over?

Then in the last light of fading day, Jake caught a glint in the snow ahead. Cautiously he approached, bent over, and with wet woolen mittens pulled it from the ground. The sight was so incongruous he stared at it for a dozen breaths before realizing what he had.

"What is —" Pierre came up close enough to see. He stopped cold, whispering, "Nom de Dieu!"

"Gold," Jake whispered. And it was. A solid gold cross, as heavy as his pistol, attached to a thick gold chain and studded with gemstones. "Gold."

Chapter Two

"Your first day on the job," Colonel Beecham said, bristling. "What happens? First you run down the best secretary in the Sixth Army right outside my door."

"Sir, I can —"

"Then you hook up with this French johnny, go gallivanting out in the woods in the exact opposite direction from where your responsibilities lie."

"I can explain, if you'll just —"

"Then you start an international border incident by leading an entire squad right smack dab into the middle of an ambush."

"— let me tell you —"

"And wind up the day by picking a treasure out of the snow and getting the wind up of the entire division."

"Please listen to my side of the —"

"Not to mention the rumors you've stirred up. The last thing I heard, it was a treasure chest so big it took fifteen pachyderms to cart it home. Don't ask me where you found fifteen grown elephants in the middle of the Black Forest. Left over from Hannibal's crossing, I suppose." Frosty eyes riveted him to the far wall. "Well? What've you got planned for this evening. An invasion of China?"

"Nossir," Jake surrendered.

"Glad to hear it. Did you bring that good-for-nothing malcontent Servais with you?"

"He's just outside, sir."

"Bring him in."

Jake hastened to the small annex one door down from the colonel's office, where he found Pierre leaning over Sally Anders' desk. Pierre straightened from his position and wiped the smile off his face as he caught sight of Jake's pallor. He followed Jake back to the colonel's office, marched smartly through the doorway, saluted, and announced, "Captain Pierre Servais, reporting as ordered, sir!"

"Cut the malarkey, Servais," Beecham snapped. "I've got about as much time for you as I do for your friend here. Now what were you doing out on patrol?"

"Checking out some new men, sir."

"Don't you have sergeants for that work?"

"Not really, sir." Servais turned serious. "I lost four just this week on postings back home. And the requests for men to be promoted to fill their places haven't been granted yet."

"Who's got the paper work?"

"Sir, I believe —"

"Morrows!" the colonel bellowed.

"Sir!" The corpulent sergeant appeared with a speed only possible for someone dedicated to listening through keyholes.

"Find out where the promotion papers for Servais' men are. And if there's any holdup, tell whoever's responsible that I've been meaning to find volunteers to test our new paper parachutes."

"Right away, sir."

"Okay, now listen up, you two." Beecham swivelled around and glared at them. "For your information, the war's over and they've stopped pinning medals on anybody who moves. If either of you two yahoos tries another end run like this, I'll use you as tent pegs! Understand?"

"Yessir," they said in unison.

"Now, where's the contraband?"

"With Morrows, sir."

"Good grief, man." Beecham was genuinely exasperated. "You don't have the brains the good Lord gave a gnat, do you?"

"Yessir, I mean, nossir."

"Leaving gold with Morrows is like asking a rabbit to take care of some lettuce for you. Sally!"

The auburn head appeared in the doorway. "You rang?"

The colonel's voice softened. "Be a sweetheart and go chase up our good sergeant. Tell him I expect to have the cross on my desk, chain and jewels intact, or I'll personally stake him out for tank target practice."

"Only if you give me first shot," Sally replied, and left. Jake thought he had caught a glimmer of sympathy as she glanced his way, then decided it was just his imagination.

"All right, listen up, you two. Your responsibilities are to liaise with the Americans and the
incoming French. This does not include skipping
out for a light fling in the snow after lunch. Nor
has anybody told you to pretend there are Nazis
behind every bush and go marching off to war
in the woods. Is that clear?"

"Yessir."

"Don't let me hear about any such collision
courses from either of you, not ever again. I hate
to lose good officers. Now get out of my sight."

"How are we supposed to liaise with troops
if we can't go out in the field with them," Burnes
grumbled.

Servais, his elbows propped on the bar and
his head down almost level with his glass, gave
a restricted little shrug. "Send them love letters,
maybe."

Jake swiped a hand over his head. "I thought
for a minute there I was going to get scalped."

"That's why they call him Smoke Beecham."

"As in, where there's Beecham there's fire?"

Servais shook his head. "As in, dragon's
breath. After Beecham passes, all that's left is
a tiny puff of smoke."

"He seemed nice enough when I first talked
with him."

"The colonel must have wanted something,"
Servais mused.

"He did."

"Like what?"

"He wants me to stay on. Or so I thought this afternoon."

Servais straightened. "Speak of the dragon himself."

Jake rose from his slouch just in time to hear the gravelly, "Evening, boys. Give me the usual, Tom."

"Yessir, Colonel."

"Can I buy you soldiers a round?"

"Thank you, no thank you, sir," they said together, still at attention.

"Forget the parade ground razzmatazz for a minute and come join me in the corner," he ordered, and walked over to the far table. Reluctantly they picked up their glasses and joined him. "Siddown. That's it. Sure you won't take up my offer?"

"I'm fine, thank you, sir."

"Well, maybe later." Beecham's easy-going manner carried no suggestion of the earlier roasting. "All right. We've got maybe fifteen minutes before the crowd arrives. Tell me what you think about your little forest run."

"Colonel," Jake looked positively pained at having to go through it again. "I'd just as soon —"

"Listen to me, gentlemen," Beecham said, leaning up close to them. "That little speech wasn't meant for you. Well, not entirely. I've got to make sure you keep your priorities straight. But what I had to make plain to my staff was that I won't put up with any bozos turning into treasure hounds."

35

"It wasn't anything like that at all, sir," Jake protested.

"I know that, son," Beecham said kindly. "I knew it as soon as I heard you'd left the cross with Morrows. That was a mistake, though. Big mistake. I thought I'd have to use a tire wrench and some dynamite to pry his grubby little mitts loose."

Beecham leaned back and waited for the bartender to set down his drink. "Thanks, Tom."

"Welcome, Colonel."

"Morrows' not the only greedy little so-and-so on the base," the colonel continued. "And that's our problem. There's no harm in telling you the truth. Not now, anyway. As long as I can rely on you both to keep your traps shut about it."

"I think I'll have that drink after all," Jake said.

"Tom! Bring over a couple of whatever they were having, will you?"

"Right away, sir."

"Rumor has it that the Nazis had a big stash of treasure around here somewhere," the colonel said quietly. "It wouldn't surprise me, since the SS used this city as their personal country club. Nor does it astonish me that we haven't found anything. Have you been into Badenburg yet?"

Jake shook his head. "I've just been in Germany a little over a month, sir. The only town I've seen is Oberkirch."

"That's not much more than a village," Bee-

36

cham replied. "And not too badly hit, if I recall. Son, Badenburg ain't no more."

"Bad," Servais confirmed quietly. "Very, very bad."

"Supposedly there are over thirty thousand people living in the ruins," Beecham continued. "Personally I just don't see how. There doesn't appear to be three bricks standing together. Not enough shelter to keep a dog dry. But you'll see it for yourself soon enough, I suppose. Karlsruhe's supposed to be as bad, though I haven't seen it for myself."

"Worse," Servais said softly. "Same ruins, more people."

"What I'm trying to say, gentlemen, is we've got more important things to do than go traipsing off into the countryside looking for lost treasure. Now, I'm pretty sure I can count on you two to keep your heads over this. But I *know* the same can't be said for a lot of the others on my staff. Do you follow?"

"Yessir."

"They had to hear me come down on you two, and come down hard. It was the only hope I had of keeping order." Beecham grimaced. "The problem isn't restricted to the lower ranks. My aching back, I wish it was. Word has it that the general in charge of the Freiburg area has got three squads doing nothing but scouring the area for Nazi loot. I'm not in the fingerpointing business. But my problem's the opposite. I've been given an impossible duty, and only a quarter of the men I need to do it with. As long as this situation continues I'm going to come down hard on anybody who doesn't have his nose to the grindstone."

Beecham took a long swallow. "But that doesn't mean you boys can't continue looking around as long as it's on your own time. And as long as you keep it quiet."

Jake permitted himself the first smile of the evening. "Quiet as church mice in slippers, sir."

"Right. Now tell me what happened."

Interrupting each other in turns, they related the events of the afternoon. When they had finished, Beecham sat lost in thought for a time, then asked, "So you think it was two men?"

"Not at first," Jake replied. "The shot came from the direction he was running in. But the more I think about it, the more I'm sure he didn't have time to turn and aim."

"It couldn't have been just a lucky shot?"

"Maybe," Jake said doubtfully. "But I don't think so."

"As hard as he was running," Servais added, "it would be tough to hit anything without taking a couple of breaths to quiet down."

"So it really was an ambush," Beecham mused.

"I figure more like a last line of defense," Jake said. "If he gets in trouble he runs toward somebody stationed at a certain point —"

"Who shoots down my men," Beecham growled. "I don't like it. Not one bit."

"Jake's not sure he was actually shooting to

hit," Servais interjected.

"What's this?"

"Just a hunch, sir," Jake replied. "But it was a high-caliber bullet, I'd know the sound of that shot anywhere."

"Sniper?"

"That was my guess. Pierre's men didn't find a second set of footprints. It would have been hard to miss them in fresh snow. I figure maybe he was stationed in a blind, and in our haste to follow the running guy, we missed the obvious."

"Not so obvious at all, Captain," Beecham said approvingly. "So he bought his man a few seconds of time with a well-aimed miss."

"Enough time for him to evade us," Servais said. "And it would have been no more than another escaped black marketeer, except for the cross."

"The cross, yes," Beecham agreed. "How do you think he lost it?"

"I saw the sack catch on branches a couple of times," Jake said. "That's how I got up as close to him as I did."

"Close enough to see him clearly?"

Jake shook his head. "I only know he had to be a young man to run that fast. Dark hair. Gray sweater and pants, or at least that's how they looked in the light. Never saw his face."

"So the cross fell from a hole in his sack."

"Unless someone else dropped it," Servais offered.

"That's possible," Beecham replied. "But

doubtful. If this is an established routine, they might use the same track. But for a man fleeing to run directly over the same piece of ground as the last man in the snow, at dusk . . ." Beecham shook his head. "It's extremely doubtful."

Beecham tasted his drink and looked up. "How trustworthy is this sergeant-major of yours, Servais?"

"An excellent man, sir. One of the best."

"So leave him and his squad on patrol duty in that area for a while. Let's wait and see if they spot anything more."

"Should I warn him to look out for anything in particular?"

Beecham gave a humorless smile. "Given the circumstances, Captain, I seriously doubt if your men will be caught napping in that area for a long time to come. Just make sure you ask him about footprints."

"Yessir."

"Sir," Jake said. "Could I ask what is going to happen to the cross?"

"Why, soldier, are you getting money hungry all of a sudden?"

"Nossir, well, that is —"

Beecham waved the matter aside. "They've got forms for such things now. And routines."

"I can imagine," Servais said. "Bye-bye cross."

"One of two things will happen," Beecham went on. "They'll put up notices, and if anybody comes forth and shows a legitimate claim to it, then back it goes."

40

"Which is unlikely," Jake said.

"In the extreme, son. Unlikely in the extreme. If it's Nazi loot, which would be my guess, then for all we know it came off the neck of the bishop of Cairo, or Persia, or the back side of Tibet. Anyway, there'll be a little wait, then the assessors will make an evaluation and give you a reward."

"Buy us off," Pierre translated.

"The reward is about a tenth of the estimated value, the last I heard. Which ought to be something. To keep the peace, I'd advise you to take a third of it and split it among your men."

"That's a good idea, sir," Jake said, recognizing an order when he heard one.

"The paper work will take six months or thereabouts, maybe longer. By that time your boys'll be scattered to the wind. Be sure and get everybody's home address, Servais."

"Yessir, I'll see to it tomorrow."

As the colonel rose to his feet he clapped Jake on the shoulder, leaned over, and said, "A word to the wise, soldiers. Sit with your back to the wall from now on. You're going to be a lightning rod for every jerk suffering from an acute case of greed."

"But all we found was the cross," Burnes protested. "And you have that now."

"You know that and I know that," Beecham answered. "But the boys slavering over these rumors are going to wonder."

"About what," Servais demanded. "Sir."

"About whether or not you two didn't pull

41

this one out of the ground because it had already been seen by the squad, then neatly kick a pile of snow over the rest."

"What rest? There wasn't anything —"

Beecham held up a hand. "There doesn't have to be. They only need to think there is. Or might be. Even one chance in a million will be enough to have them gathering like a pack of wolves after a kill."

Beecham straightened up. "You both should take anything of value you have in your room, give it to Sally, and let her lock it in the company safe. And as I said, guard your backs."

At the sound of other voices echoing down the hall from the Officers' Club, they rose to their feet with one accord. Servais led Jake out and down the side stairs and over to where his jeep was parked. No word was spoken. None was necessary. They weren't ready to face the prying eyes and probing tongues just yet. The colonel's warning was too fresh.

Pierre barreled along the road back to the main camp at what Jake considered kamikaze speed. So when they rounded the curve and saw a mobile checkpoint right in front of them, it was too late to stop.

Pierre scattered the MPs like so many white-topped bowling pins, and only missed ramming through the barrier by doing a four-wheel spin that carried them within inches of the MPs' jeep.

In the momentary stillness following their icy

halt, Jake recognized a few faces among the soldiers picking themselves off the ground. He only had time to whisper, "Trouble."

"You know them?" Servais murmured back.

"Unfortunately."

"Well, well, well." The MP closest to the jeep was a tough-looking sergeant, about as pliant as a tank barrier. "Hey, boys, look who we've got here."

A voice from the darkness said, "If it ain't our old friend Captain Turncoat Burnes."

"Out in the dark all by hisself," said another shadow. "Except for another dang foreigner. Not German, though. Whassa matter, Captain Turncoat, did the Krauts at the camp get tired of playing your games?"

"You boys been playing much football lately?" Jake asked quietly.

"Here and there, Captain. Here and there. We missed having you around for a rematch, though. Ain't that right, boys? Pity how the camp league was disbanded all of a sudden like that. But I guess you knew all about that, huh, Captain Turncoat."

"No," Jake replied quietly. "I hadn't heard."

"Musta happened the day you left. Yeah, we and the boys were just talking about how tragic it was you had to leave us all of a sudden like that."

"Compliments of your friend," Jake said. "Colonel Connors."

"Yeah, well, he might be our friend, Captain

Turncoat, but he sure ain't yours." The sergeant's gaze shifted. "That your Frenchie driver? Whoever he is, he just about made meat pies outta my men."

"The name is *Captain* Servais to you, Sergeant."

"Hey, boys, get a load of how the Frenchie here parlays the lingo." The gaze remained settled on Servais. "As for trying to pull rank, Frenchie, it's after curfew, nobody's out, and we're miles from the base. Which means there ain't a soul to hear you squeal when my boys take you out back and give you and Captain Turncoat here a little driving lesson. Compliments of the house." Dark eyes gleamed in the lantern's glow. "That is, unless you boys got something real nice to tell us."

"What are you talking about," Servais demanded.

"He means the cross," Jake explained. "News travels fast around here."

"That kind of news sure does," the sergeant replied.

"There isn't any more treasure out there," Jake replied flatly.

"Now that's a real pity," the MP said. " 'Cause my boys are real eager to get on with the driving lesson, and I can't hardly see any other way to keep them under control."

The barrel-chested sergeant took a step back and joined the solid phalanx of men surrounding the jeep. "Now are you boys gonna come quietly, or do we start our lesson in safe road habits right here?"

Jake stiffened for the lunge, but before he could do more, Servais was up and moving faster than Jake thought possible.

Instead of rushing the men who were directly beside his door and thus prepared, Pierre leapt up and over the windshield. He raced down the hood, screaming like a banshee, and crashed into the two startled men in front of the jeep. A pair of blows that were little more than a blur, perfectly aimed for the point where jaws joined necks, and the men went down like felled trees.

The small man vanished into the darkness, still screaming.

"After him!" the sergeant yelled.

But as the circle began to break up, before there was a leader or a clear sense of direction, Servais was back, still yelling. He leapt up so high his body rose above the head of the first attacker, so high he kicked *down* on the man's head. Touching earth, he spun like a top and planted a flying boot alongside the second man's face. He met the oncoming fourth with hands like blades. In two strokes he stood over another body.

Jake broke his own stillness with two bounding strides, quickly covering the distance between himself and the sergeant, and put all his speed and weight into flattening the man's nose. The sergeant howled, grabbing his face with both hands.

45

Then a baton landed on Jake's shoulder, and the ground rushed up to meet him.

He caught sight of Pierre falling beneath a trio of baton-wielding MPs, and was tensing his body in anticipation of the next blow when headlights came up from the other side of the barrier and shone full upon the tableau.

The door to the saloon car opened and shut. A pair of lightstepping shoes approached. Nobody moved. Everyone was as frozen as the night.

A woman's voice rang out, "What's going on here?"

The voice was answered by silence, save for some heavy breathing and a few soft groans. "You, Sergeant!" Sally Anders' fury rang in the crisp air. "I'm speaking to you! What's the meaning of this?"

The big man rose from his crouch, attempting with one hand to stem the red tide flowing from his nose. His voice was clogged and his face pale in the headlight's beams. "They were resisting arrest, ma'am."

"That's absolute rubbish and you know it. I've heard all about your football game, Sergeant. As has Colonel Beecham, in whose jurisdiction you're now standing, and who is waiting impatiently for the urgent papers I'm delivering."

The sergeant pointed over to where Servais lay prostrate on the snow-covered ground. "Ma'am, that Frenchman was driving like a lunatic. Almost mowed me and my men down."

"No doubt a safer tactic than being stopped

and mobbed by you thugs," she snapped back. "Now if you want to carry on a grudge match one-on-one, Sergeant, that's your business. But a vendetta with twenty against two will not only cost you your stripes, but earn you passage home in the brig." Her voice was an angry lash. "Do I make myself clear?"

"Yes, ma'am," the sergeant muttered.

"Now back off. All of you! Captain Burnes, are you able to drive?"

Jake lifted himself with difficulty, his shoulder throbbing. "I think so, ma'am."

"Some of you men lift Captain Servais into the jeep. Move!"

"I'm all right," the Frenchman said in a slurred voice, struggling to his feet.

"Have your men lift this barrier. Now, Sergeant! I haven't got all night." Sally started toward her car, then spun back and snapped, "And if there is one more incident, if just one hair on either of these officers' heads gets mussed in any way, by anybody, at any time, I will report to Colonel Beecham that I witnessed a bunch of MPs assault a pair of superior officers. He will then personally see to it that each one of you spends the next few years where you belong — in a hole!"

After Sally's door slammed shut, there was a moment's silence, then, "Whattawe do, Sarge?"

"What the lady said," he replied dully. "Open the gate."

"But, Sarge —"

"Just do it!"

Jake eased himself behind the wheel and started the motor. When the sergeant stepped forward, Jake faced him squarely and said, "You and your boys never could play football."

The big man tasted bile. "We'll get you yet, Turncoat."

"Doubtful, doubtful," Jake replied, ramming the gears home. "Brawn doesn't make up for lack of brains. Not on the field, and not in life."

They followed Sally's car back to staff HQ in silence, enjoying the feel of the wind, the sense of ease between them, even the aches of their bodies. They were alive! The thrill of combat was one never to be forgotten, never sought, but when there, it was incomparable. Alive!

Sally drew up in front of the HQ building, got out and waited for them to stop. In the jeep's headlights Jake realized that the woman's face was wet with tears. He turned off the motor and jumped out, instantly solicitous. But she cut his gesture short. "You two are nothing more than a pair of animals!"

The onslaught was so unexpected he had no defense. "I — what?"

"Haven't you had enough of war?" Her shrill voice split the night. "How long will it take for you to see the evil behind all this violence?"

"Wait. They were the ones who —"

"I don't *care!*" she screeched. "All I want is for it to *stop!* I thought you were different. Caring enough to help the German soldiers regain some self-respect, build up morale, but you're no dif-

48

ferent from all the rest of them! You can't fight the Germans anymore, all the fight's been beaten out of them. So now you've got to find somebody else to fight."

"That's not it at all," he protested, taking a step forward.

"Yes it is, and don't you dare come near me! Those men out there are supposed to be on the same side as you! And what were you two doing? Going after them like the combat soldiers you are! Go look at yourself in the mirror, soldier. Aren't you just spoiling for another fight? That's all you're really good for, isn't it? Isn't it?" Sally turned and fled into the quarters.

Jake watched her depart, then turned back and slumped into the jeep. Servais eyed him with a jaundiced air and said through bloody lips, "If I were you, my friend, I believe I would cross her off my list."

Chapter Three

Two days after the night attack, Jake Burnes entered the central Karlsruhe HQ to the sound of applause.

The Karlsruhe army staff was split into a dozen different segments, as no building large enough to house everyone had survived the war. The main headquarters was contained in a requisitioned two-story office complex which had somehow escaped unscathed, while its neighboring factory had been reduced to a two-acre dust heap.

Staff housing was a routine problem, causing the same set of predicaments throughout all Germany. As 1945 gave way to 1946, there were over a million American soldiers struggling to police their segment of a destroyed nation, and waiting with growing impatience for orders to be shipped home.

No longer was there the unifying goal of victory. Victory was theirs. The time of celebration had passed. The horrors of discovering the concentration camps were behind them. The Nuremberg Trials had begun. A new routine was being established, that of victor ruling over the vanquished.

Four nations had substantial forces occupying Germany — France, Britain, Russia, and the United States. A number of others were also represented, from Greece to Denmark, Belgium to Australia, South Africa to Canada. The Four Powers gathered and argued continually. Stalin was proving almost impossible to deal with. His demands rankled more and more each day. Even as far away as Karlsruhe, on the other side of the country from the gathering Soviet troops, people were on edge whenever Stalin's name was mentioned.

But the biggest practical problems were unrelated to the high-level diplomacy. The infighting among the tightly concentrated forces around each base was ferocious. Command posts had to be split up and spread out across cities and regions, roads were scarred and pitted, and working telephones were as rare as fresh eggs.

Finding allies for any undertaking, especially one as peripheral as joining another nation's forces to help guard a border no longer under attack, was essential. Liaison jobs had to be handled like nitroglycerine.

Knowing all this added mightily to Jake's surprise over the reception he and Pierre received.

As Jake let the door shut behind Servais, he turned to find the cluster of officers clapping and whistling for the pair of them. They exchanged astonished glances as a man with major's pips walked up with hand outstretched. "Major Dan Hobbs. Let me be the first to congratulate the men who took Connors' gorillas down a peg."

Jake accepted the hand, but quickly confessed, "Actually, it was the lady who saved the day."

"Yeah, we're taking up a collection to send the Ice Queen a wreath." The major grinned. "Tell me you didn't have the whole thing timed."

"We didn't have the whole thing timed," Jake agreed.

"Then somebody's fairy godmother was working extra hard that night." Major Hobbs clapped Jake on the back, said, "Come on into my office, gentlemen."

Once his door was closed, the major said, "Connors is making himself an impressive list of enemies."

"I didn't know he was so well known," Jake said.

"How long have you been in these parts?"

"Just over a month," Jake replied. "Transferred up from Italy."

"So you arrive, get together a squad of prisoners and whip Connors' pride and joy from here to Moscow."

"I sort of inherited the team," Jake explained.

"Then you dig up the first whiff of treasure —"

"Like you said," Servais said to Jake. "News travels fast in these parts."

"And then proceed to whip his goons a second time."

"It came close to being the other way around,"

Jake pointed out. "How did you hear about it?"

"One of my men was up at Badenburg and caught sight of the Ice Queen laying you two out in front of HQ. So did Colonel Beecham. Colonel Beecham ordered her to tell him what happened, as she wasn't all that eager to have it spread around. My man overheard the story." Major Hobbs grinned. "Man, I wish I'd been there to help you guys out."

"We could have used it, sir."

"Skip the sirs, it's just us turkeys here anyway. You know Connors is scouring the forces stationed around here, trying to dig out all the toughest guys?"

"I guess that news missed us."

"Yeah. He's putting together a rough crew. Sort of his own private army. The other MP officers around here can't stand him. They won't allow Connors' boys even to set foot into their territory. That's why he agreed to play touch football with your team. Nobody else'll touch them with a ten-foot pole."

"They were big," Jake said. "But they were dumb. It wasn't that hard to out-think them on the field."

"So I heard." The major's good cheer clouded over. "We're hearing some rumors that they've worked over some people. Way outside the line of duty. Nothing proven. Just stuff passed down the road."

The idea burned a hole in his gut. "I thought the war was over."

"Yeah, that's what I heard too." Major Hobbs' gaze turned sharp. "I've even been wondering if there might not be more than bullies at work here."

"I don't follow you."

The major focused on Servais. "You've been around here for a while, haven't you, Captain?"

"Almost six months, sir. Since just after VE-day."

"Had you ever seen a roadblock at that point before?"

Slowly Servais shook his head, knitting his brow in concentration. "Now that you mention it, nossir. Nowhere near it."

"Strange place to set one up," Major Hobbs went on. "Out in the middle of nowhere, forest around on every side, only traffic that time of night probably between the base and headquarters down the hill. Makes you wonder."

"Do you think they set up an ambush for us?"

"You said it, not me, soldier." The major played at casual. "Just the same, I'd watch my step if I were you."

"That's exactly what Colonel Beecham told us."

"Yeah, there's no water on the colonel's back. If he said something like that to me, I'd pay attention. Now, what was it I could do for you gents?"

Jake explained his official mission. "We'd like to ask you to assign men to patrol the border as far as Wissembourg to the north and Rastatt to the south."

Major Hobbs stood and walked over to the large map on his side wall. After a moment's inspection, he said, "We're talking about a forty-mile stretch, give or take a dogtrot."

"That's about it, yessir."

"I guess I've got no problem with that." The major came back and sat down. "I'll have to run it by the brass, but I doubt they'll object. There's a lot of respect for Beecham around these parts. What are we supposed to be on the lookout for, anyway?"

"Displaced people, escaped POWs —"

"Guys carrying sacks of treasure on their backs," the major added.

"Does everybody know about that?"

"Well, I couldn't tell you for sure, but my guess is that by now they're discussing it at the White House. Sure as little green apples it's festering in the brain of every one of my men."

"It was just one cross," Jake objected.

"This time," Major Hobbs observed. "Goodness only knows what might pop up next time, am I right?"

"I suppose so," Jake said glumly.

"Well, don't you worry, Captain. I'll make it perfectly clear that the first soldier of mine who turns trigger happy with the scent of treasure goes home in handcuffs."

"Hello, soldier." Sally Anders seemed neither pleased nor displeased to see him. "What brings you here?"

55

Turning his cap over in his hands, Jake entered her small cubbyhole. That she merited a private office was the clearest possible indication of her prestige. Her desk was piled high with forms, official-looking documents, and buff-colored envelopes marked Priority. "I don't know whether to say thank you or I'm sorry."

"Why, soldier, are you feeling guilty about something?"

"You saved our lives back there," Jake said. "And for that I'm grateful."

"I don't know about your lives," Sally replied. "But I did save you from a beating."

"Those goons wouldn't have stopped until we were a couple of bloody pulps."

She made round eyes. "Those nice men? Do you really think so?"

"This is hard enough, Miss Anders. Could you maybe hold the jokes until I'm through?"

"Sorry." She folded her hands over the papers nearest her. "Proceed, soldier."

He took a breath. "I'm not saying I agree with what you said out there on the street. But I want to tell you how sorry I am that I —"

"Neither did the colonel," Sally interrupted. "Agree, I mean. He got the story out of me in the end, you know. I never was able to stand up to him in a fight. He was pretty angry that I hadn't let him kick the colonel and his men from here to Cincinnati. But he did call Connors this morning and give him a good roasting. He told the colonel the only thing which saved him was that I refused to testify against his boys so long as you two remained intact. I think you should be safe."

Jake remained silent, his eyes on his hat.

"Oh, I'm sorry. I interrupted your groveling," Sally said, all mock sympathy. "Do go on, Captain."

"You're going to make this as tough as you can, aren't you."

"No reason not to. You're too big to turn across my knee, and a piece of my mind won't help things a bit. Might as well make you squirm."

Burnes started for the door.

"Jake!"

Reluctantly he turned back. Sally said quietly, "You really shouldn't give in so easily, soldier."

It was Jake's turn to show surprise. "Ma'am, if you think I'm giving in, you've got another thing coming. This is what we combat soldiers call a strategic withdrawal."

Sally inspected him for a long moment, then came to some internal decision of her own. "Have you got your jeep?"

"Right outside. Why?"

She rose from her chair. "Take me into town, will you? There's something I'd like you to see."

"Sure."

She pointed to a group of burlap sacks piled in one corner. "Give me a hand with those."

Jake walked over and hefted one. "What's in them?"

"Contraband, soldier. Don't ask so many questions."

They made the trip in silence, Jake because he was too wary of being shot down again, and Sally because she seemed to prefer her own company. Directions were passed on with the minimum of words or a simple hand movement.

Their route took them down what had once undoubtedly been a major thoroughfare, now a broad strip of cracked and pitted pavement bordered on both sides by rubble. The surroundings were as gray as the sky.

Not a single building was intact. As far as Jake could see, the world was filled with single walls jutting like crumbling fingers toward an uncaring sky. All open spaces were filled with bricks and mortar and the refuse of war. A thick layer of dust covered everything.

The people they passed seldom looked their way. Attention was almost always focused downward, as though no one cared to see much of their world. There were a few bicycles, but most people straggled aimlessly by on foot. The only cars they passed bore military markings. On almost every street corner a man stood with a sign saying in German, "I must eat. I will do any work. Please help me."

At several crossings, gangs of street kids materialized from thin air and chased after them, calling out for candy, cigarettes, chocolate, or just calling. Jake had seen this kind of thing in the smaller village where he had been stationed before, but had never grown accustomed to it. Every child he saw appeared to be begging. And here there were so many of them. All skin and bones and ragged clothing. And eyes. Haunting eyes big as saucers and old as war itself.

They stopped in front of what probably had been a prestigious apartment block, now a flattened heap with two intact walls and a free-standing chimney. Jake could see a few pictures, washed-out wallpaper, and water-stained curtains hanging from the interior of destroyed apartments.

He parked as Sally directed and followed her down a set of stairs into what had previously been a neighborhood bomb shelter. The door of the low building was marked with a broad painted cross. From the interior rose the sound of children chattering and playing.

On the bottom step Jake hesitated, his forehead creased in thought. Sally turned around. "What's the matter, soldier? Afraid of a few kids?"

Jake shook his head, unable to figure out what had surprised him so. He followed her into what appeared to be a crudely painted fairy tale kingdom. The walls were decorated with bright sketches of stories done with an amateur's hand — Jesus on the Mount, walking on the water, calming the storm, healing the leper, gathering the little children. In the far corner stood a makeshift communal kitchen. Beside it stretched a long table with benches. The ceiling was oppressively low. Without the wall murals the chambers would have been grim.

"Jake, I'd like you to meet Chaplain Buddy Fox."

"Any friend of Sally's is a friend of mine, Captain." The chaplain was a small man with sandy hair and a voice as gentle as his eyes. "Welcome to my little crèche."

Jake snapped his fingers and declared, "Laughter."

"I beg your pardon?"

"Laughter. I've been trying to figure out what it was about this place. It's the first time I've heard laughter off the base since," he tried to remember and was sobered by the realization. "Since I arrived in Germany."

"That's the chaplain's doing," Sally said quietly.

"I'm afraid we don't have much in the way of refreshments, Captain. The children devour everything just as fast as it arrives."

"Cookie's sent you some more supplies," Sally said. "We'd better get them out of the jeep before somebody makes them disappear."

They went back upstairs and pulled out the sacks from the back of the jeep. Chaplain Fox peered into the first one and said, "Please tell Cookie how very grateful I am," he said softly. "And the colonel, of course. Without them —"

"They know," Sally said. "We all do."

"This is a wonderful place," Jake said as they returned to the shelter. Eager little hands reached out for the sacks, but not with the imploring, demanding, frantic plea that met him everywhere he went outside. Here it was a game. "Really wonderful."

"Why, thank you, Captain. Here, just bring the sacks back to the pantry, will you? The only way I can ensure that we make our supplies last is to lock them up. I have no idea how children normally are at this age, but these are eternally hungry."

The several dozen kids all appeared to be under six. The youngest were still in diapers, gathered on a pair of stained mattresses by one side wall, watched over by a trio of young girls involved in some intricate hand game. A gray-haired matron sat on the floor surrounded by children, keeping them quiet with stories. Another woman watched over some children playing with battered building blocks and a few other toys. As the sacks were set down and the storehouse door relocked, the women's gazes remained fastened intently on Chaplain Fox.

Jake looked down at the children. "Whose are these?"

"Buddy's," Sally replied. "Chaplain Fox's."

"Well, there are several local people who help out," said the chaplain. "We have worked out a series of shifts, and pay what we can from these stores. No one really has enough to eat, you know. Many such women are quite happy to work for food, and we need as much help as we can afford. I still have my divisional duties, of course. But everybody helps as they can. Some with food, others with blankets, a few with chocolates and cigarettes and other things I can use for money. And then Sally and Colonel Beecham help with everything possible, from medicines to stores to paint for these murals."

"I mean," Jake said, "whose kids *are* these?"

"Nobody's," Sally replied.

"God's," Chaplain Fox corrected. "As are we all."

"I'm beginning to believe you," Sally said. "Sometimes, anyway."

"Nothing on earth could give me greater pleasure to hear," he said.

Jake asked, "Are all of these orphans?"

"A few of them, but not too many," Chaplain Fox replied. "Not anymore. Orphans are being gathered by church organizations, the young ones anyway. No, these are the unwanted."

"Kids kicked out of their homes," Sally explained. "The ones left to fend for themselves. They fall through the cracks of officialdom, because their parents are still drawing rations for them and legally, at least, they still have a home."

"They're just left on the streets?"

"Or in trash cans," Reverend Fox replied, smiling sadly. "Or at train stations. Or on rubble heaps. Some the local gangs bring in, now that they know we are here."

The chaplain caught sight of Jake's expression. "Do not be too harsh on the parents, Captain," he said. "Some are genuinely good people who have come to realize that under the present circumstances, they have no way of bringing in enough to keep their entire family alive. So one must be sacrificed for the good of all. Sometimes it is the youngest, sometimes the one who causes the most trouble, sometimes a sickly child, or one who appears to be a little slower than the others."

"This is awful," Jake murmured.

"This is war," Chaplain Fox replied. "This is why we need God. Here. Everywhere." He smiled at Sally. "And the grace of friends like this dear lady."

"You supply the love," Sally replied. "I'll see what I can do about the grub."

"God supplies the love," Fox countered gently. "And the healing. If you look, I wager you'll find there is quite enough of both leftover for you."

Sally turned toward a group of a dozen or so young girls who had been quietly waiting for her attention. She squatted down and was swiftly enveloped by small arms and questioning voices.

Reverend Fox brought Jake back around. "You are Sally's friend?"

"I'd like to be," Jake replied.

"She needs a friend," he said, inspecting Jake with clear eyes. "Come with me, would you?"

Jake followed him back out into the cold winter air. "She's got walls high as the Matterhorn."

"Yes, she has." Buddy Fox offered a smile. "Just the sort of challenge for a strong man like yourself, I'm sure. Are you married, Captain?"

"No."

"Girl back home?"

"Not anymore."

"Ah. A casualty of war." He motioned toward someone behind Jake. "There goes yet another casualty, one I see much too often these days."

Jake spun, caught sight of a gang of young teenagers flitting around a corner and vanishing. "They're outcasts too?"

"Almost all children of that age are left to fend for themselves, at least to some degree," he replied. "Most of them have no fathers. Fathers are a rare commodity in Germany these days. Whole adult men of any age are, for that matter. An entire generation is growing up void of role models and direction, Captain. If only I had a division of strong and caring men like you. I just might be able to reach them."

As Sally came through the doors and up the stairs toward them, Jake asked, "Do you have any contact with these kids?"

"With several of the local neighborhood gangs, yes, as a matter of fact, I do. We offer them meals two afternoons a week. It is both a peacekeeping measure, and a way of learning who they are. Many of them are growing up like wild tomcats, constantly on the prowl, sleeping where and when they can."

"For some of them," Sally said, "the only kind words they ever hear are the ones Buddy speaks to them."

"If only there were some way to fill their empty days," the pastor said worriedly. "If only I could

64

give them a *purpose*. They need that as much as they need more food."

Jake was about to express his sympathy over the plight of the young Germans when he was suddenly struck by an idea. He stood there, his mouth open, wondering how on earth anything could feel so right.

"Is anything the matter?"

He gathered himself, shook his head. "Let me go check on something," he said. "Maybe I can give you a hand with the kids."

Chapter Four

"You want me to do *what?*"

The colonel's roar echoed through the open door, stopping all typewriters, footsteps, and conversations within hearing range. Jake pleaded, "It's just a gimmick, sir."

"It's absolute madness, is what it is!"

"I'm not looking for results, sir," Jake persisted. "I'm just trying to give them something constructive to do with their time."

"You call running loose on the streets constructive?" The colonel's voice was loud enough to shake the windows three doors down. "This is what my liaison proposes is the best use of his time? Maybe I need to remind you, mister, that I could always make you officer in charge of the spud detail!"

"They're already running loose, Colonel," Jake replied as Beecham stomped over and slammed the door. "And as far as I heard, they live pretty much full time on the streets as it is."

Colonel Beecham walked back around his desk. "You've got to stop doing this to me, Burnes."

"Doing what, sir?"

"Putting me in a position where I should blow my stack. It's bad for my blood pressure." Beecham slumped back into his chair with a sigh. "You ought to know better than to come in and propose such a scheme in full earshot of everyone."

"I guess I wasn't thinking, sir," Jake replied, not understanding at all.

"No, that's one thing I'll agree with right off the bat. Maybe nobody heard you. Then again, maybe Morrows had some urgent filing that left him loitering just outside my doorway as usual. You know how it is. Anything to do with treasure, and this whole place threatens to come apart at the seams."

"I'm sorry, sir. It's just —"

"I know. I know." A glint of humor appeared in that steely gaze. "Buddy's got you hooked too, has he?"

"Sir?"

"Buddy Fox. The chaplain. He's gotten under your skin, has he?"

Jake nodded slowly, and confessed, "I heard them laugh."

"Yeah, that hit me below the belt too. Never knew I could get so much pleasure out of such a simple sound. Or miss it as much as I did when it was gone." Beecham fiddled with his pen, then gave an abrupt nod and said, "Okay, son. How much do you need?"

Jake's hopes soared. "As much as Stores can spare, I guess, sir."

"Well, you sure can't bring them here and have Cookie dole out the leftovers. Not unless you want to make us a laughing stock from here to Berlin."

"I can't?" Cookie already spooned out leftovers at the outside gate every evening to the people waiting there. They were always waiting, and there was never enough.

"Good grief, son. Did you really think you could line up a dozen young kids out there day after day and not have the word leak out? No, strike that. Word is bound to get out anyway. But can you imagine what they'd be calling us if we lined them up here?"

"It's more than a dozen, sir," Jake interjected.

"Even worse. The Burnes Blarney Brigade. Or maybe Beecham's Best. How'd you like to hear that every time you turned around?"

"I guess I hadn't thought it out, sir."

"Don't get me wrong, Captain. Your idea has merit. Anything that might help some of these kids needs to be taken seriously. But we've got to present it in a way people can accept. Do you understand?"

Jake nodded. "Just another hand across the waters."

"Now you're thinking. All we're doing is helping to feed a few of the older kids. Nothing more, nothing less. Everything else stays between us."

"And Captain Servais," Jake added.

"And the chaplain and Sally. Those two wouldn't give Connors and his goons the time of day. But around everyone else except them, lips are to stay permanently zipped tight."

"Mum's the word, sir."

"You just make sure those kids understand they're not to take any risks."

"From the looks of things, just being alive out there is risky," Jake replied.

"No additional risk, then." The gaze showed grudging approval, but all Beecham said was, "Still bucking for another medal, aren't you?"

"Nossir, that's not it at all," Jake answered, rising to his feet. "As you said, Colonel, I'm just trying to feed some hungry kids."

Captain Servais was still out on patrol. Jake stopped by the supplies division, known far and wide simply as Stores, then drove back into town alone.

When he walked through the crèche door, the first person he saw was Sally. "What are you doing here?"

"That's what I like about you, soldier," she replied, hands on hips. "You really know how to make a girl feel welcome."

"Is the chaplain around?"

"Why, hello, Captain." Chaplain Fox stepped out from behind a curtained alcove. "What can I do for you?"

"Cookie asked me to drop off some supplies," he said, hesitant to discuss the real reason behind his visit.

"Why, thank you, Captain, but we're not scheduled for another shipment until Thursday."

"We'd better get outside while there's still something to unload," Sally reminded them.

As they left the crèche, Jake said softly to the chaplain, "I need to talk with you. Privately."

"Just take that satchel on back to the storeroom, dear," Chaplain Fox said. He waited until she walked back down the stairs, then asked Jake, "What's on your mind, Captain?"

As swiftly as he could, Jake outlined his plan. The chaplain inspected Jake with a new appreciation.

There was a scraping sound. Jake turned around and discovered that Sally had remained standing on the bottom step. "I thought you were taking the things inside."

"Don't get hot, soldier," Sally said mildly. "I think it's a good idea."

"You do?"

"So do I," the chaplain told him. "There should be no difficulty increasing our meals to the children from two to five times a week. We pay our cooks with food, you know. I'm sure they would be happy to take on the extra work."

"You shouldn't call them children," Sally said, her eyes still on Jake.

"No," Chaplain Fox agreed. "I suppose I'm looking at the size of their underfed bodies, not the depth of their experience. They've packed a lifetime into a few short years. Some of them, several lifetimes."

"I don't know how long the support can last,"

Jake warned, thinking of his own impending departure.

"Anything that will help these young people stay alive and out of harm's way through the winter must be taken seriously, Captain."

"Call me Jake."

"Thank you, Jake. Yes, in times like these, seeing to the needs of today are as far as anyone can afford to look."

"So you think it will work?"

"It's not what I think, but whether they will accept it that is important." The chaplain hefted two bulky sacks. "Let's get these stores inside and go find out."

Jake picked his way across a stretch of shattered pavement as treacherous as river ice cracked by spring thaws. Over one million tons of bombs had been dropped on German cities by Allied planes during the last few months of the war. Few buildings were left intact, and inner city roads were treacherous in the extreme, especially now with their covering of frozen snow and slush.

Civilians walked and slid and stumbled wearily across the uneven sea of snow and ice and dirt. Those with bicycles pushed them along, not letting go for an instant — with the scarcity of transport, bicyclists lived under the constant burden of envy and the threat of theft. Nobody met Jake's eyes. Wherever he looked, eyes dropped immediately to the ground. But he felt their gaze on him always, everywhere.

71

They crossed a plaza whose once majestic central cafe was now a three-sided empty hulk. They were surrounded by windowless buildings whose empty eyes stared in dark and silent sorrow. From time to time Jake caught sight of families huddled within. Their only protection from the bitter weather was an occasional rag or blanket tacked over a hole. Wood was too precious as fuel to be used for boarding over the buildings' wounds.

"Whatever you see," the chaplain told Jake as they walked, "don't let the children sense your reaction."

"Why not?" Jake watched a group of elderly people being directed by a loud-mouthed overseer. They sifted through the ruins of a collapsed building, collecting bricks. These were piled into wheelbarrows and rolled to a corner of the square where the oldest women squatted and hammered off the clinging cement. The bricks were then loaded onto a single waiting truck. Everyone moved in the slow motion of the almost starving.

"I'm not sure," Chaplain Fox replied. "They just hate being looked at. Maybe they expect you to be disgusted as others have been. Maybe they want a reason to dislike you. Maybe it's shame. Maybe it's despair. I have simply found it best not to notice how they are forced to live."

He led Jake through a building entrance that had been tripled in size by a direct hit. The bomb had taken out the floor, revealing a deep basement far below. A beam too heavy to steal had been laid across the pit. Jake could see how at night the beam was dragged back and secured with wire cable, offering a wartime sense of security. Jake followed the chaplain across, his hands out and wavering.

The building's single intact chamber was redolent of cocoa. Chaplain Fox halloed through the makeshift entrance cover, then said to Jake, "This used to be one of the city's finest chocolate factories. It specialized in handmade pralines. That is why these children are able to claim it for their own. Two other families used to live here, but in their hunger the odor almost drove them mad. It has not been any better for the children. Since they moved in, I have had to take three of them to the hospital after they ate dirt which had collected the scent. Still, I suppose it is better than sleeping out-of-doors."

The tattered burlap curtain was thrown back, revealing a sunken-cheeked youngster of perhaps fifteen. He peered at the chaplain with undisguised hostility, then turned and shouted back into the chamber, *"Es ist der Pfarrer und ein Fremder."* It's the priest and a stranger.

"Lass denn rein," came back the reply.

Jake stepped gingerly into the gloomy depths. The only light came from a smoldering cooking fire and from around the burlap hanging over the single window. Better dark than freezing, he supposed. The room was marginally warmer than the outside.

Fox's German was surprisingly good. "Where is Karl? I have someone he needs to meet."

"The only person I'll ever need to meet is the devil, Pfarrer," a voice sounded from the gloom. "Isn't that where you say I'm headed?"

"I pray not," the pastor replied, untouched by the unseen man-child's anger. "This friend has an offer for you."

"Your friend, not mine," Karl scoffed. "Tell him we take whatever we want, with or without his offers."

"This one you'll like," Jake said for himself, pleased that he had managed to speak in a flat, unconcerned tone. He ignored Fox's startled glance at the sound of his German. "It'll give you something besides dirt to fill your bellies with."

"So, so. An invader who knows the mother tongue." A tall lanky youth, skinny to the point of emaciation, stepped from the shadows. "What do you have that could interest me, *Fremder?* Chocolates? Cigarettes? Where is it? In your pockets? Yes? You like me to search them for you?"

Jake stood his ground. He met the young man's hostility with a flat gaze. "You've got spunk, I'll give you that much."

"You'll give me nothing," he spat. "You'll give me death. That's what you'd like, yes? To see us all just curl up and die."

"Food," Jake replied. "Three times a week. Hot. Fresh. Add that to the two meals the chaplain is already giving you and there's a chance you might survive this winter after all."

The anger faltered momentarily. "You lie, *Fremder*."

"That is something I will try never to do," Jake said solemnly. "I will even start with truth. There is a chance this will only last for five weeks. But five weeks is better than nothing."

Other boys and girls emerged from the dimness, coalescing into wasted rag-draped shapes that appeared to be little more than hollows and eyes. Their eyes were huge. Great, dissipated eyes, large as saucers, that stared unblinking at Jake. Food.

"Hot meals," Jake repeated. "And something else you need to make life worthwhile. Something else you need almost as much as a home."

"What is that, *Fremder?*" But without the resentment this time.

Jake looked straight at the young German, and replied, "Hope."

"You want us to do your searching for you, is that right?"

Jake sat on a stone across from Karl, surrounded by silently listening wraiths. It was hard to tell the girls from boys, and not simply because of the dim light. Emaciation had stripped their bodies of muscle and feminine contours, and turned all faces into almost identical sets of hard lines and deep hollows. "There will be two groups," Jake said, explaining the plan he had outlined to the chaplain. "While your gang looks for smugglers, the others will search for some place large enough for a hidden hoard of treasure."

"Who is in this other group?" Karl demanded, turning to the chaplain. "The Crypts?"

Fox nodded in the affirmative, explaining to Jake in English, "The other gang I work with lives in an abandoned cemetery. Well, abandoned is not the right word. Stuffed to the gills and then left alone is more like it. They found an old mausoleum, broke in and stripped it bare, and are living there now."

"In my chambers the only language spoken will be my language," Karl insisted.

"Of course," Fox said. "It was a slip. Forgive me."

The unexpected courtesy stopped the youngster. Jake recalled Sally's comment that the only source of kindness for these children was the chaplain. Jake said, "What I need from you is your help in finding the people shipping the treasure across the border. I suppose it would be possible for your gang to search out information for me?"

Karl puffed out his gaunt chest. "We go where we like, when we please. We hear and see and know everything."

Jake rose to his feet. "Then it sounds like I've come to the right place."

"One moment, *Fremder*." Karl remained seated on his little rock throne, the room's single chair covered with several layers of sacking for comfort. "Why should we tell you anything? Why not just keep it all for ourselves?"

"Where would you go with treasure?" Jake countered. "Who could you trust to pay you anything, give you anything except a knife across your neck?"

There was a murmur of agreement through the room. It was the only time anyone else had spoken since their arrival. "And we can trust you?" Karl asked suspiciously.

"I bring you food," Jake pointed out. "And you know the chaplain's an honest man."

"I trust him to do as he says," the chaplain affirmed. "I think you should as well."

"We will discuss your offer, *Fremder*," Karl declared.

"Then come for a meal tonight," Fox replied. "Thinking is easier with a full belly."

On their way to the cemetery, Jake confessed, "I don't see how you can deal with this on a daily basis."

Fox made his way around an ice-encrusted bomb pit. "I just put my trust in the Lord and go where I feel called."

"But doesn't it get to you?"

"Of course it does. But I can't let it crush me. I wouldn't be able to do my job."

"I don't understand how you do it."

"There is sorrow everywhere, Jake. Everywhere and always. A man has three choices — any man, chaplain or otherwise. He can let it overwhelm him, and if he does, it will drive him around the bend. We've both seen cases of that, haven't we?"

"Too many," Jake confessed.

"Yes, that is the tragic nature of war. The product of war is ruin, of cities and of lives. Peace is only a by-product. A wish. A goal. That is why war must always remain an instrument of last resort for any civilized nation. But where was I?"

"Choice number two."

"Yes. The second alternative when faced with the agony of war is to lock yourself away. This the majority choose to do. Nowadays we are seeing thousands of men who simply refuse to leave the base except when on duty. Others do leave, but all they allow themselves to see is their hunger — for sex, for drink, for some gratification or another. Still others see nothing but their own hate. They remain blinded at will, and view their own pain and anger as justification for a nation's suffering."

"Are they wrong?"

"I try not to judge anyone, Jake. But I think their lives are misery. They remain imprisoned within themselves. God holds the key, of course. With forgiveness. With love. With compassion. And with healing. But only if they ask for it. And to ask they have to recognize their internal prison for what it is. That I see as my job, to be a mirror for anyone struggling to look with honesty. To help them see the lies they tell themselves for what they are."

They detoured around a building that had slipped from its destroyed foundations and created a hillock in the middle of the road. When they reached the other side, Jake asked, "And the third?"

"The third choice is to learn to take each day as it comes, and to do what you can with what you have. This means learning that you cannot avoid seeing the suffering of others, which is hard. Extremely hard. I would imagine that it would be impossible to do this without the strength of God in your heart. At least a believer can respond to this suffering with prayer. But the key is to learn to do with what you have, Jake. That is the central issue. Do not see yourself as a failure because you can't touch all who suffer. Recognize that universal healing can only come through Jesus Christ, and accept your assigned task. Then do all you can with everything you've been given."

Chapter Five

They returned from the second meeting to find Sally Anders still at the crèche. Jake walked through the door and was met with the cocked head, the hands on hip, the blunt, "Well?"

"Well what?"

"Don't be obtuse, soldier. How did it go?"

Chaplain Fox answered for him. "It went splendidly. I do believe they have taken to both Jake and his idea."

Jake fumbled about with his cap, bent over to stroke the cheek of a passing little girl. Finally he glanced back at Sally. She watched him with a small smile playing across her lips. "You may invite me out to dinner, Captain Burnes," she said. "If you like."

"I like very much," he said.

"I know a little place not far from here. A farmhouse. Probably the only decent restaurant for miles. You can pay with dollars, chocolate, cigarettes, booze, or food."

"Sally, I think you should know I didn't do this for you. Well, not entirely. That is —"

"I know, I know," she said, reaching for his

arm. "That's why I accept."

Jake pushed open the crèche door, waved a farewell to the smiling chaplain, said, "Step into my Rolls, and let me take you away from all this."

"If only you could, soldier," Sally said, mounting the stairs. "If only you really could."

They climbed a hill out of the city, passed through deep forest as darkness descended, then came over a crest and entered a clearing that stretched out for what seemed like miles. A cluster of farm buildings offered the only sign of life. The farmhouse was a vast structure, rising among a series of stables and barns that covered over an acre. Lit by lanterns and warmed by a sweet-scented wood fire, the farmhouse was the first sign of coziness Jake had seen in months.

"This is terrific," he said, taking his place at the end of a long farm-style trestle table. "How did you find it?"

"Being one of the few American women around means I field all kinds of offers," Sally replied, settling herself across from Jake. "You should know that, soldier."

Seven long tables filled what once had been a great family hall. Antlers and old blunderbusses decorated the high smoke-stained walls. The farmer and his wife, serious middle-aged folk, cooked and served with the help of a pair of shy country girls. The clientele was mixed. A few German civilian officials who had the power to obtain curfew passes sat in shiny suits beside women decked out in hats dating back to the thirties. They spoke in low whispers and avoided the eyes of everyone else. Most of the others were American officers from surrounding garrisons. Some escorted local girls. Those without female company sat in inebriated clusters and eyed the others with envy.

Sally's beauty drew a lot of stares. The candlelight flickered with gentle fingers across her face, deepening the glow in her eyes, softening her features. It even seemed to gentle her voice. "There's no menu," Sally explained as the host walked over and set two pewter mugs and a tall clay jug in front of them. "Homemade brew to drink, and whatever dish they have."

"Schweine Roladen mit getrokene Pfifferlingen und Knödeln," the host said abruptly, *"Zwei Dollarn pro Kopf."*

"I only got the first couple of words of that," Sally admitted.

"Ist gut, wir nehmen zwei Portionen," Jake said for them both, then translated when he had left, "Pork loins rolled and stuffed with smoked ham. Pfifferlingen are mountain mushrooms, sort of nutty tasting. A lot of country people pick them in the fall and hang them out to dry. Knödeln are big potato dumplings."

Sally shrugged out of her jacket, a stiff affair meant to copy a uniform's uncompromising lines. Underneath she wore a starched white blouse which accented the delicate curves of her body.

Her hair was pinned back, but enough had escaped to fall in abundant auburn disarray around her shoulders. "Where did you learn your German?"

"I was studying at the university when I was called up," he said by rote, then stopped himself. "That's not exactly true."

She leaned across the table. "Are we going to be truthful tonight, soldier? Sounds dangerous."

He ignored the jibe. "My brother was already in the infantry. Nothing was ever said about it, I guess there was no need to. After I finished my second year at university, I enlisted. That's just how things were. The last thing my dad told me was, be a good soldier. I was brought up to obey my parents. I did as I was told."

"Where are you from?"

"A small town nobody ever heard of. Sauderton. Pennsylvania. Dutch country. Solid people. Hardworking. Bedrock of the nation type of folk. The kind who go where they're told and do what they're told to do."

She inspected his face, and said, "Are you looking forward to going back?"

Slowly Jake shook his head. No.

"Why not? The decorated war hero coming home to a grateful nation. They'll have a parade for you, Jake. Make all kinds of speeches."

"Parades come to an end," Jake replied quietly, his eyes fixed on the fire. "Speeches go where all hot air goes."

"Why don't you want to go home?" Sally pressed.

"I'm just kind of lost, I suppose," he said quietly. "Here or there doesn't seem to matter so much, when 'there' is no longer the place I left behind. People and places change, I stay the same." He turned to face her. "Lost here, lost there, what's the difference?"

For some reason his words had stripped her bare. It took a while for her to gather herself, then she asked, "What is it you're after?"

"I don't know," he sighed. "Things just seemed a lot clearer in the war. Everything came down to one basic rule — knock out the enemy. That was the only way to survive."

"Weren't you scared?"

"I lived with fear all the time," he replied. "Every time we were about to go into action, I used to get such a sick in my stomach until the first shot was fired. Then all that mattered was surviving. Keeping myself and my troops alive, and bringing the boys home."

"And so now you miss it."

"No," he stated flatly. "That's not it at all. I know some guys do, and I can understand them. I really can. But that's not the way I feel."

"What is it, then?"

He wrinkled his forehead in concentration. "What I did stood for something. I fought for what I believed in. There was a clear pattern to life. That much about it felt good. I was doing something with meaning. Now it's gone. All gone.

84

I guess I just need something to believe in."

Sally filled their two cups, lifted her own, and said, "Here's to all the yesterdays, soldier. Wherever they've gone."

"To yesterday," he agreed.

"I want it all back. All of it. I'd trade my life for one day of how it used to be." She set down her cup and said softly, "I can't work out how it's supposed to be now."

"I can't either," he agreed.

Their meal was served, two steaming platters piled high with solid country cooking, German style. They ate in silence, gathering themselves, recovering from the shock of honesty.

Eventually she set her fork down with a contented sigh. "I didn't know how tired I was of army food, or how much I needed that meal, soldier. Thank you."

Jake nodded. "Will you do me a favor?"

"Depends."

"Stop calling me soldier."

The look of mock surprise returned. "All this time and I didn't notice? Excuse me, sailor. I didn't catch the cut of your uniform."

"Not sailor, either," he persisted. "Jake. Just Jake. It's my name."

"Okay, Just Jake. From now on, Just Jake, that's all you'll hear."

"Why do you make a mocking joke out of everything?"

"It's my last line of defense," she said, her tone brittle. "Don't knock it down. Please. It's not much, but it's all this girl's got left."

He searched her face and said quietly, "Tell me about your fiance."

Her eyes became open wounds. Her mouth worked, but for a moment she could manage no sound. Then, "Why?"

"Because I want to know. Because I feel his presence with us here."

"No you don't," she said shakily. "What you feel is his absence. He is not here. I wish he were, but he's not."

"Tell me," Jake pressed.

She turned away from him and looked out beyond their table, beyond the farmhouse wall and the darkened forest and the dusty tumble-down city and the war-torn country, to a place and a time that was no more. Jake let her be, content to sit and watch her search the unseen distance, and wonder if a woman would ever love him that much. Or if he would ever deserve such a love.

She turned back and said with strength and a kind of fervor, "He was a great man, Jake. Not a good man. A *great* man. The hardest thing I've ever had to do in my whole life is forgive God for letting him die. Sometimes I can, and sometimes it's just beyond me. I mean —" She stopped and took a couple of harsh breaths. "The world needs men like him, Jake."

"Tell me about him," Jake asked, because it seemed now that she wanted the question asked. It tore at him more than he thought possible to encounter this love for another man in her voice and her eyes. But still he asked.

"Strong," Sally replied, smiling with a tenderness that washed over him, making it hard not to stand and rush over and crush her to his chest.

"Strong in body and strong in spirit," Sally went on, unaware of the effect she was having. "He was a leader. Not born that way, but made that way through his faith. All the credit for his life he gave to God." Sally looked at him, but saw him not. "I've never met a strong man who could be so humble. I admired him. I admired him as much as I loved him."

"And you loved him a great deal," he said softly.

"More than my own life," she said, her voice trembling. "More than . . . More than I thought it was possible to love and lose and survive. But I did. Lose him and survive the loss. For the longest while I didn't think I would. He taught me to see God as somebody alive. That was an incredible gift, his ability to make the unseen seem within reach. And now that he's gone, I can't find that invisible strength when I need it most."

"But you've made it."

"In a way. I almost didn't, though. I almost accepted the fact that this old body would keep right on ticking for another fifty years or so, but the life would be gone. Dead and dried up and blown away."

"What changed your mind?"

"The children," she replied simply. "Seeing others who hadn't ever had the chance to live and love at all suffer a hell as bad or worse than my own. It woke me up, Jake. It made me realize that I had a purpose too. It gave a meaning to what was left of my life. But I had to make a choice. I could either drown in my sorrow and watch my soul die, or I could struggle back to the surface and survive. Or try to. And I did. But I didn't do it for me. I would never have had the strength to do it for myself. I did it for them."

She toyed with her cup, her eyes downcast. Jake waited quietly. At that moment, he would have been willing to wait for her all his life, and still count himself lucky. Then she said softly, "If only I could find my way back to what he taught me about the Invisible, maybe I could count my life as worth living again." She looked at him. "Do you think it might happen?"

"I don't know," Jake replied quietly. "I've never been much of a believing man myself."

"He would have liked you, Jake," she said, the tender smile returning. "He used to say that strength wed with wisdom was God's most underrated gift."

"I don't think of myself as particularly strong," Jake countered. "And I don't rank high in wisdom."

But she chose not to hear. "It's so easy to talk about God when I think of him," she mused aloud. "And so hard otherwise. I wish I could understand why."

Chapter Six

The next morning, Servais was ebullient over Jake's scheme. "A masterpiece," he declared. "A stroke of genius."

"Just trying to feed a few kids," Jake said.

"Nonsense. You wait and see, my friend. This will benefit not only your young charges but us as well."

"They don't have a chance in a million of finding treasure, and you know it," Jake protested.

"I was not speaking of the treasure," Pierre answered. "Not just, anyway."

"What do you mean?"

"Let us wait and see," he replied. "Come. This is an important meeting today, and we must not be late."

The incoming French forces had established an initial base of operations next to the Rhine. The great river began high in the Swiss Alps, ran up through Germany, and ended its twelve-hundred-mile journey off the Dutch coast. It also formed the border between France and Germany from Basel to Karlsruhe, a distance of some one hundred miles. To the west of this border lay the province of Alsace, over which the Germans and French had fought for more than two hundred years. To the east loomed the Black Forest foothills. The river jinked and curved and split and tumbled over drops. The skeletal remains of bombed-out bridges grew giant icicles and stood as silent memorials to the recent war.

As Pierre set his customary blistering pace down the rutted road, he filled Jake in on the situation confronting the local French patrols. Boats were being intercepted nightly. The vessels were usually loaded to the gunnels with contraband or displaced aliens. These would-be immigrants wandered throughout Europe, in search of a better life. Their final destination remained unclear. Anywhere was better than the bombed wastelands of Eastern Europe, now occupied and stripped to the bone by Soviet troops. Most of these refugees were half-starved and feverish and on their last legs. When stopped they made no protest. They had long since reached a point where they continued moving only because there was no place where they could stand still.

When Jake and Pierre arrived at the camp, they found the tragedy of these displaced persons mirrored in the deep furrows creasing Major Gilbert's features. His office was built on a rise overlooking a massive internment camp, which used the Rhine's sweeping expanse as one natural boundary. Through the windows Jake could see tall wooden guardhouses rising every several hundred meters along the river. Guards watched over the flowing waters twenty-four hours a day. Jake was unimpressed. He saw with a soldier's eye, and noted how difficult it would be to police the undulating terrain with its many curves and crevices. No doubt a score of boats got through for every one caught.

The discussion between Servais and Gilbert was in French. Jake did little besides sit and look attentive. But he could tell Servais was getting nowhere. The major repeatedly shook his head, barked a reply, and flung an arm toward the large-scale map pinned to his wall. The response was clear. Until more troops arrived, the major was doing the best he could.

Pierre sighed in defeat, paused, then launched into a gentler assault. This time the major softened. And softened further still. Dark eyes turned in Jake's direction. The major tut-tutted in time to Pierre's words. Jake struggled not to squirm under the major's gaze, and wished he knew what was going on.

"*Les pauvres garçons,*" the major said when Servais had finished his tale. "*Et les filles. Les filles!*"

"I informed the major about your little project," Servais murmured in an aside.

Jake nodded, concealed his alarm, and said conversationally, "If Colonel Beecham hears about this he's going to roast us both over a slow fire."

The major launched into a hand-waving exposition, full of sighs and headshakes and liquid gazes into the distance. "The major has three children around that age," Servais translated. "It breaks his heart to think of what those hundreds of children must be suffering."

"Strike that," Jake said. "It's fifty kids at the outside."

Pierre gave his head a minute shake. "I found it necessary to employ a bit of literary license."

"Meaning?"

Pierre shrugged. "I lied."

But the major was already up and moving for the door, ushering them along with urgent gestures. Reluctantly Jake allowed himself to be led down a well-worn path toward a trio of warehouses lining one side of the camp. As he walked, Jake glanced over the wire barrier and into the internment camp. His look was returned by a thousand watchful, silent gazes. Bearded men. Kerchiefed women and girls. Boys in oversized caps and ill-fitting clothes. All with a vague sense of alienness that marked them as Eastern Europeans. All with a stillness borne on pleas so intense that no words spoken to a stranger could hold them. At the warehouse entrance Jake returned the guard's salute, and entered behind Pierre and the major. Inside he found organized pandemonium.

At their end, supplies from a pair of trucks with red crosses stencilled on sides and back were being unloaded by jostling, sweating, shouting men. In the middle section a group ran to and fro, all carrying clipboards and pens, all pointing and shouting and counting and waving frantically for attention. Farther back, yet another group sectioned big piles of clothing and supplies into much smaller piles, tied them with string, and shoved them on — all the while sweating and screaming and pointing and grabbing for more of this or that. At the very far end, a calm group passed on the little tied parcels to a seemingly endless line of waiting refugees. With each package went a few kind words in a language most of the refugees did not understand. Jake thought the entire scene looked extremely French.

The major immediately leapt into a swearing match with the two truck drivers. The pair gave as good as they got, at least in the beginning. But gradually they were whittled down to sulking submission. When the major turned away, the drivers retreated behind stinking French cigarettes and serious scowls.

"The major regrets he can only offer us the use of these two trucks," Servais translated, wearing a lopsided grin.

"For what?" Jake demanded.

"My friend," Servais said around his rictus grin, "I would strongly advise you to bow and give solemn thanks."

Major Gilbert wheeled about and paraded down the aisle, throwing grandiose gestures at the wealth stacked up around him. Pierre hustled alongside, dragging Jake with him, and translating, "All this has been entrusted to me for those in need. Inside or outside the wire, what does it matter? I feel I can trust you to give to those whose life might depend upon the giving. This trust is a rare and precious thing, and one which should be built upon."

Jake protested, "What about the refugees? Don't they need this stuff?"

The major stopped, and replied solemnly through Pierre, "My detainees are being seen to. They are receiving clothes and food and medicine and shelter. The greatest of their needs, however, is not to be answered by what you see here. They need a home. They need freedom. They need a regime where they do not have to live in fear of the knock on their door. They need a country where the sky does not rain death."

Gilbert gave a magnificent shrug. "Alas, these things I cannot offer. So I feed the bodies, and hope that someone will arrive soon with a way to feed their souls."

Moments later, Jake and Pierre were in the jeep on their way back to base, followed by their convoy of two borrowed trucks. "How could you do a thing like that?" Jake demanded.

Servais was all innocence. "Like what?"

"Make the major think I was playing Pied Piper to a townful of kids."

"Amazing what a desperate man is capable of," Servais replied. "Until I hit on that, I was afraid the only way I could crack his armor was with a mortar shell." For a change, Servais was keeping his speed down to a level that did not leave Jake gritting his teeth and hanging on for dear life.

The pair of trucks grinding along behind were incapable of faster speed, loaded as heavily as they were.

"Only now it's gone from three dozen kids to three hundred," Jake complained. "I could throttle you."

"I would advise you not to try, my friend."

"Yeah, I saw what you did to Connors' goons. What was that?"

"In North Africa, I fought with a man from Thailand. A Frenchman by birth, but he had lived most of his life in Indochina. He taught me."

"It's impressive to watch."

"For a while we weren't sure they were going to let us fight in the war," Pierre said. "De Gaulle was always arguing, arguing, and for the longest time all we did was sit around and try to gather news of what was happening. The waiting was terrible."

"I've never been any good at that either," Jake said. "Waiting."

"So he offered to teach me," Pierre continued. "Which helped pass the time. It was not easy to learn."

"It doesn't look easy. As a matter of fact, it looks on the wrong side of impossible."

"That is my specialty," Pierre replied. "Doing the impossible."

"Great," Jake said, stretching out as much as the jeep's cramped confines would allow. "Then we'll just let you be the one to sell the colonel on this."

Colonel Beecham scowled as they appeared in the doorway to his office. "Not you two again."

"Promising," Jake murmured. "Very promising."

Pierre began, "Sir, we have had —"

"Don't stand out there like a couple of bell-boys," the colonel snapped. "Come in and shut the door."

"Yessir." Pierre scowled at Jake's barely repressed grin as he turned to shut the door behind them. Keeping himself rigidly erect, he started over, "Sir, we —"

"Keep it short and sweet, mister," the colonel barked. "And whatever it is that you're aiming to work up toward, the answer is no. I've got too much going on to get involved with whatever fun and games you two have thought up now."

Jake covered himself with a discreet cough.

"Sir," Pierre persevered, "we have received the support of the French garrison commander, Major Gilbert, for our children's relief project."

"So?" The colonel's attention was already being drawn back to the papers littering his desk.

"I, ah, believe Chaplain Fox is a little short of storage space just now," Pierre said delicately.

"So go see Stores," Beecham said. "Why are you bothering me with this?"

"Yessir." Jake spoke for the first time. Before Pierre could open his mouth again, Jake grabbed him by the shoulder and spun him around.

"Thank you, sir. Sorry to have troubled you, sir."

But before they could get out the door, Beecham said, "Just a minute."

"Almost home free," Jake murmured.

"Come back in here and shut that door." When they had done so, Colonel Beecham demanded, "Exactly what kind of support are we talking about here?"

"We're not quite sure, sir," Pierre replied.

"Not sure? Not sure of what?"

"Well, you see, sir, the major got sort of impatient when they were loading the second truck, and sort of took over himself. After that, they just threw in whatever they grabbed first."

Colonel Beecham leaned away from his desk and said quietly, "Second what?"

"Truck, sir." Pierre motioned lamely toward the unseen front of the building. "Parked just outside, sir."

"You have two *truckloads* of supplies?"

"Yessir."

"Whose life did you mortgage for that payload, mister?"

"Nobody's, sir. You see, the major has three children —"

"Stop right there," Beecham snapped. "I am absolutely positive I don't want to hear any more of this. Just tell me one thing, mister. Is any of this payload stolen?"

"Nossir."

"Contraband?"

"Not a bit of it, sir."

"You haven't passed off a paymaster's chit?"

"We didn't have to sign anything, sir."

"Sort of manna from heaven, is that what you're trying to tell me?"

"I suppose you might put it that way, sir."

"Get out of here, both of you. And if you know what's good for you, you'll steer clear of me for the next few days. You hear what I'm saying?"

"Loud and clear, yessir."

"Scram."

They swept through the door at lightning speed, closed it softly, breathing a silent sigh of relief. Then they caught a hint of noise from behind the colonel's closed door. It sounded like a chuckle. Jake formed a question with his eyes. Pierre frowned and shook his head in reply. Not possible.

In the hallway, Jake said, "I'm thinking."

"Don't make yourself feverish," Pierre warned.

"I'm thinking we could use some reinforcements for breaking into Stores," Jake said.

Pierre considered the idea. "Sally?"

Jake nodded. "Come on, let's see if she's around."

On the way down the hall, Pierre asked, "Where were you until after curfew last night?"

"Don't ask."

"Sally?"

"I told you, don't ask." They walked on in silence, then Jake said, "She was right, you know."

"About what?"

"About us wanting to turn that little confrontation the other night into a battle. We didn't even try to work out a peace."

To his surprise, Pierre did not contradict him. "That is the trouble with women, my friend. They are often right. Too often for their own good." He inspected the man walking alongside him. "You like her, yes?"

"Very much," Jake confessed. "Maybe too much."

"Yes, I am liking her too. She is not only beautiful but smart enough not to be trapped by her own beauty. That is a rare trait, my friend. Very rare."

"She also has walls a hundred miles high."

"Ah, but every wall must have a door." Pierre grinned. "The question is, which one of us has the key?"

Sally was both there and available to help. She gave no sign to Jake that anything had taken place between them the night before, and treated Pierre's suave banter with polite disdain.

The trucks, however, brought a rise. When she had walked around them both, peered into the open flaps, smiled a greeting to the still disgruntled drivers, she walked back over and asked, "So who did you kill?"

"It's a gift," Jake said.

"The first of many," Pierre boasted.

Jake cast him a dark glance and said, "The silver-tongued devil here to my right told a French major that I was taking responsibility for

99

the safety of several hundred kids."

"Well," Sally declared, "we can't make the gallant captain into a liar, can we?"

"What do you mean by that?"

"Let's find a place to stow these riches, then go have a talk with the chaplain." Sally climbed onto the running board of the first truck and pointed it forward and around the corner.

Stores was contained within its own private compound, and protected by its own guard contingent. Assignment to guard duty within Stores was one of the most fought-after postings in all Germany. Which Stores did not matter. Each was a gold mine of opportunity. Even the lowliest of privates assigned to Stores possessed an air of smug sleekness. Access to Stores meant a ready supply of trading goods, and in the broken-down economy of war-torn Germany, anything could be had for a price. Anything at all.

The Stores major was a banker in uniform, and wore an expression that remained constantly on the verge of saying no. He was singularly unimpressed with Sally's request for help. "Much as I'd like to help you, Miss Anders, I'm afraid storing your items here is absolutely out of the question."

"It's just for a couple of days, Frank. For goodness' sake, you're bound to have some corner you're not using."

"That's not the point. We simply can't set this sort of precedent. You're a bright girl, I'm sure you understand what I'm saying. We're talking about principle here."

Sally leaned across the desk, her eyes flashing. "I'll give you principle, you pompous stuffed shirt. I've got sixteen loads of goods on requisition right now, just waiting for the colonel's signature. It's a shame the paper work is about to get buried. For about ten years."

"You can't do that," the major protested.

"You just watch me." She held his gaze long enough to drive the point home. "Now please march outside and find us a nice, dry corner. And keep it well separated from any of your own stuff. If I catch any of your sticky-fingered mutts nosing around our goods, I'll make sure your next shipment of cigarettes winds up in Siberia."

While the goods were being unloaded, Sally went off and returned with two able-looking enlisted men, and posted them on either side of the supplies. She also made a hand-lettered sign and pinned it to the first stack of boxes. The sign read, "If you're found here tonight, you'll be found here in the morning."

"What's all this?" Jake demanded.

"Insurance." She turned to her two men, raised a finger, and said in a stern voice, "If anybody comes within fifteen paces, you are ordered to shoot."

"Sure thing, Miss Anders," said one of the men with a grin.

"I'll arrange for you to get some extra time off once we've got all this squared away," Jake promised.

101

"No problem, Captain."

"Yeah, sir," the other agreed. "We think it's great the way you're helping these kids."

Jake shot Sally a glance. She shrugged. "What can I say? Word gets around."

"Come on," Pierre said. "Let's go find the chaplain."

They drove back to the base, found Chaplain Fox in his office, and explained the situation to him. But he refused to take charge. "You seem to be doing a fine job on your own," he said.

"We haven't done anything but scare up a few supplies," Jake protested. "You have the contact with the kids."

"You have just as much influence with them as I do," he replied. "The colonel has been after me for shirking my base duties. I am afraid, my friends, that this is one ball you will have to run with yourselves."

Once they were all back outside his office, Jake asked, "What do we do now?"

Sally was already putting on her coat. "Do what the chaplain says, what else? Let's go scare us up some kids."

Jake managed to find his way back to the destroyed chocolate factory. Even though the gang had already received its first free meal, the greeting was no warmer than the last time. "What do you want, *Fremder?* We don't have anything for you yet."

"That's not why I'm here," Jake replied quietly. There was a fiercely pathetic air about the place. An air of defeat and impending death made their bravado all the more tragic. He worked at keeping his face blank.

"Brought a few of your little friends around?" Karl demanded. "Take them for a visit to your own private zoo?"

Servais stepped forward. "Perhaps I can help."

"No!" Karl shouted. "Here you will speak the mother tongue and nothing else!"

"My friend speaks no German," Jake said.

"Then he can leave! Him and the female too. We want nothing to do with you, *Fremder*, not you, not your friends, not your pity."

But Servais was not to be put off. He murmured, "Pep talk."

"I —" Jake stopped. "What?"

"Follow my lead," Servais said swiftly, then stomped to the center of the room, threw his hands up in a dramatic gesture, and roared out a torrent of words. In French. Which Jake did not understand at all.

The boys and girls watched him open-mouthed. When Pierre paused for breath, Karl asked, "What is he saying?"

"He, ah, he is speaking of the future," Jake managed. He was saved by another deluge of words from Servais, who had adopted the regal manner of a general addressing his troops, and did it well. So well, in fact, that even Jake found himself drawing up a little straighter.

103

When Pierre stopped the next time, Jake was ready. "The French officer has taken time from his extremely busy schedule to come and personally pass on very important information," he translated. "He wishes you to know that your bravery in the face of enormous difficulties has been brought to the attention of the highest authorities."

Servais was off again, using the enormous voice of one accustomed to speaking to a division drawn up for formal inspection. It held the youngsters spellbound. At the next pause, Jake continued. "We come to you with a new mission. One which is dangerous, but which we are sure you are up to. If we did not have confidence in you, we would not have selected you for such a vital task."

Again the hair-raising torrent, and then from Jake, "We want you to make contact with every gang in the center city. Tell them we wish to speak with all of them. Do not tell them of your investigation. First they must be judged as worthy. Have them and all their members gather at the staff headquarters on the outskirts of town — do you know where it is?"

"We know," Karl replied, now without rancor. Doubtful but curious. Caught up and listening.

"Tell them that whether or not they are chosen, all will be rewarded just for appearing. Including yourselves. Especially yourselves. They are to come tomorrow at dawn, just after curfew has been lifted."

Jake caught Pierre with a sideways glance, and

104

the Frenchman stopped his verbal onslaught in midstream. "It is a perilous assignment, but one worthy of your skills." Jake waited, then asked, "Do you agree?"

There was a long pause, then, "We will do it."

Chapter Seven

Dawn came reluctantly. The sun remained hidden behind a motionless veil of frozen mist. It coated every surface with a fuzzy winter's scrawl, a written warning of the four harsh months yet to come. The little group of men that Jake, Pierre and Sally had gathered stomped around, blowing into mittened hands and speculating in muted tones about whether the kids were going to show.

A sixth sense must have alerted them, because Jake could detect no change to the frozen dawn. Whatever the reason, all sound died away as though on signal, all eyes turned to search the gathering light.

With the scarcest of sounds, gray-faced wraiths began to emerge from the freezing fog. They walked with the evident fear of mongrels not sure whether a cuff and a kick awaited them. Yet they came. It was one thing to run alongside a passing train or jeep or truck or marching convoy, to beg with words and gestures, to meet the conquering soldiers on turf they knew and understood; it was another thing altogether to walk toward a place that before had meant only beatings or shots fired in the dark. Yet they came. They stumbled from cold and from hunger, they tripped on the tattered footwear that scuffed and slapped softly with each step. Yet they came.

Still the gathered men could not move. It was a confrontation that no one was ready for, no matter what they might have been told. Here was war, the small faces said in silent agony. Here was the reality of battle. Here was the hidden cost of the fighting as armies struggled against each other. Here was need.

"Welcome," Sally's voice rang out clear and bell-like in the silence. "Don't be afraid. We want to help you."

She reached with frantic hands for something, anything, to hold out, and came up with chocolate bars. She reached out with them and said in her hesitant German, "Look. For you."

Into this frozen tableau they came, slowly, fearfully, with suspicion battling hunger on their faces. Finally a scarred and dirty hand was close enough to reach out and take trembling hold of Sally's offering. Then another, and another, and another still.

As the number of scrawny hands reaching up toward Sally increased, the first ray of sunlight forced its way through the fog. Its unexpected power startled them all. Eyes squinted, hands were lifted to shield faces, and in that moment the soldiers were suddenly able to move, to act, to serve. The scene sprang to hectic life.

Pierre took charge of the handouts. Each youngster received chocolate, tins of food, soap, a blanket, an item of warm clothing. Those with rags stuffed with newspapers tied up around scrawny ankles received shoes. Each gang received a bucket, a pot, a portable cookstove, a handful of utensils. Each child heard words spoken with warmth. It mattered little that few soldiers spoke German, and fewer children understood English. What was important were the smiles accompanying the words; a few children even managed to smile back.

The men found it less and less possible to meet the eyes of the soldiers with whom they worked. There was too much emotion in the moment, too much being brought up, too much on the surface exposed for all to see. Gazes were limited to those across the line, those who waited and searched with the frank honesty of the young and the injured, those who spoke so much without saying a word.

Sally was seated on a pair of stacked cases, writing at a table made from two crates. Each gang identified their leader. Carefully Sally took down the name, after explaining over and over and over that no, she did not work with the dreaded police, and no, the information would be given to no one else. She wanted it only for sending out more supplies. Still the leaders would only give their first names. Sally accepted this condition, taking only what they would willingly give. When they saw that she was not ordering, not threatening, not insisting they answer or give back all this newfound wealth, most of them gave her everything she wanted.

Where was each gang's headquarters? In a cemetery; a bombed-out school; a bomb shelter; a cellar; a ruined bus. How many members? Ten; thirty; seven; four dozen. Did any have families with lodgings where they could have food and perhaps shelter in the worst weather? A few did, most did not. Identity cards? Almost none. To the authorities they did not exist. They were not part of the flimsy official structures, and therefore were simply not expected to survive. How old was the gang's youngest member? Fourteen; nine; twelve; seven; six; five; four.

Jake stood just beyond the fence of the supply center, assembling and addressing one gang at a time. Carefully he explained that he needed their help in an investigation. But whether or not they decided to help, they could keep the gifts. And if possible there would be more. And they were to take no risks, or no more than they were already taking. But yes, he needed their help. They could go where he could not. They could hear what his ears were deaf to. They could see into places closed to him and his men.

As he spoke, Jake caught sight of a change taking place in some of the youths — not all, but some. Their eyes caught a glimmer of something. Interest. The first shred of excitement. A shadow of pride. They were *needed.*

The process consumed more time than anyone expected. No matter how many children they dealt with, there were always more. The sun gathered strength and burned away the remaining mist, leaving the gathering in full view of all the soldiers arriving for duty. Groups gathered and clustered and pointed and stared. Eventually the Stores major came out from his office to order his men back to work, but before his words were out, he too was riveted by the sight.

And still they came. Holding back until the soldier keeping order motioned for each new gang to move forward. Not really believing it was all happening, even when the gentle words had been spoken and the wares settled into their open grasp. Their eyes searched everything with fear and hunger and pain, and seared the souls of everyone who turned their way.

Jake finished with one group and motioned the next one over, only to turn and find a thoroughly uncomfortable Stores major standing by his elbow. The man harrumphed a few times, shuffled his feet, then said, "How are your supplies holding out, Captain?"

"I've been a little busy, sir —"

"Getting low," Pierre called over. "Very low."

"That's what I thought. Let me see," he stammered, "that is, well, perhaps I might be able to find a few extra items around."

Sally filled Jake's astonished silence with, "Whatever you can spare, Frank, I'm sure would be most helpful. We appreciate it."

"Very much," Jake managed.

"Good. Then I won't be a moment." The major

110

scurried off, barking for his men to follow. In a matter of seconds a steady stream of soldiers pushing trolleys loaded to the limit were headed their way.

Jake had scarcely begun with the next gang when a familiar voice stilled the entire procedure. "Is this your doing, Captain?"

"Tenhut!" shouted a voice about five minutes too late.

Jake snapped to attention with all the other soldiers. Suddenly the children were in a state of tense readiness for flight. "Yessir, I guess it is, sir."

Colonel Beecham cast a frosty gaze over the proceedings. "How much longer do you expect to be?"

"We're processing them as fast as we can, sir."

"See that you do, Captain. We can't have these kids blocking military traffic."

"Yessir, fast as we can, sir."

Beecham scanned the scene a moment longer, then tapped his cap and said, "Carry on, then."

"Yessir, thank you, sir."

Jake permitted himself a breath once the colonel had moved off. He returned his attention to the kids. They seemed to be watching him differently. As he finished with that group and started with the next, Jake tried to identify the change. Somehow the arrival of the colonel, his words, his salute, and his departure had validated Jake's mission. They listened more carefully, believed him more readily. He found them repeating questions less, no longer expecting some hidden price. The colonel had appeared and approved. They were being recruited for something *real*.

Another half hour, and the last of the gangs had been brought forward, their arms filled, their details taken, their mission stated. Jake watched them disappear into the distance with a sense of numb fatigue.

"A miracle," said a gentle voice behind him. "One of the most incredible miracles I have witnessed in this entire war."

Jake did not need to turn around to know who spoke. "You were drafted as the contact point," he told the chaplain. "It appears that every gang in the city knows who you are."

"Seven hundred and thirty-six," Sally announced triumphantly as she walked up beside him. "Fifty-nine gangs in all."

"And we ran out of our own supplies right at four hundred," Servais said, drawing up alongside. "The rest came from Stores."

"A modern-day version of the loaves and fishes," Chaplain Fox said. "This is a day for signs and wonders."

"Ah, excuse me," a stranger said, walking up to the group. "Could I ask who is in charge here?"

Chaplain Fox pointed at Jake's chest. "He is."

"I'm Dr. Weaver. Harry Weaver. I'm a surgeon at the local base hospital. A couple of my colleagues and I were down here for a conference this morning, and, well, we were wondering if perhaps we might be able to help with your project." He motioned toward where the last of the departing children were vanishing down the road. "We thought we might be able to vaccinate them, maybe set up a clinic or do rounds for a couple of days, something like that."

"Signs and wonders," Chaplain Fox repeated. He patted Jake on the shoulder, said, "You heard the colonel, Jake. Carry on."

Chapter Eight

Pierre and Jake drove south to Oberkirch, too overcome by the morning's events to speak. They traveled in silence, their senses open and filled by the surrounding countryside. The day had turned bright and crisp, the air scented by the forest and farmland through which they passed.

Military traffic was heavy, but mostly headed in the opposite direction. The Americans were either consolidating their men and equipment into the region around Karlsruhe or moving it farther east, in anticipation of the French army's arrival.

The base was a hive of activity. Platoons were being lined up and marched into waiting trucks. Piles of equipment were checked and sorted and loaded. Men marched and shouted and whistled and gestured wildly, competing with the din of a hundred revving truck and tank engines.

The staff headquarters was set in a relatively quiet alcove, separated from the main garrison grounds by a grove of trees. Jake and Pierre were halfway down the walkway when, from the top of the HQ stairway, an all-too-familiar voice stopped their progress.

"Well, well, well." Colonel Charles Connors had a reed-thin voice that adapted well to his air of perpetual disapproval. "Could this truly be the famous Captain Burnes?"

Jake snapped to attention, his eyes straight ahead. "Morning, sir."

"Yes, I do believe it is." Connors walked down three steps, pausing on the next to last so as to be able to look Jake straight in the eye. "What a pleasure it is to see you again, Captain."

"Thank you, sir."

Connors had an undersized body encased in a blanket of lard. His thinning strands of hair were Brylcreamed and laid across his skull in a vague attempt to hide his widening bald spot. He had no chin to speak of. His eyes were a pair of pale blue marbles. His nose was a sparrow's beak, barely substantial enough to support his eyeglasses. His mustache was pencil-thin and quivered as he spoke.

"It appears that I shall be seeing more of you than either of us expected, Captain."

"Happy to hear that, sir," Jake ground out.

"Yes, I'm sure you will be interested to hear that my authority to maintain law and order has been extended to include the region around Badenburg. That is, until the French arrive, of course." The blue eyes glinted. "Which means I shall be required to keep a very close watch over you, Captain."

"Then I'll certainly know where to turn if I ever have a question about right and wrong, sir."

The colonel reddened, subsided, and turned to Servais. "And who do we have here?"

Pierre snapped to attention. "Captain Servais, sir."

"Ah, yes. The gallant Frenchman who almost cost me half a guard detail."

"The road was very icy, sir."

"Yes, what a pity. Well, Captain, I would advise you to choose your companions with greater care. Captain Burnes here is what we could class in our army as a bad influence." Connors cast a disparaging eye down the front of Jake's uniform. "There are all sorts of ways for a man without scruples to gain a chestful of medals."

"Sir, I resent —"

"Dismissed, Captain," Connors snapped. Then, as they turned away, he continued. "Oh, by the way. I'm sorry to be the one to tell you, Captain. My men were forced to arrest several of your former team for inciting a riot in the camp the other evening. In any case, they got into a fight among themselves during the night. Several of them required hospitalization, I'm afraid. It appears that this football idea was not quite the morale booster that you and others made it out to be. The Germans are enemy soldiers and must be treated as such."

"You mean your animals waded into a bunch of helpless prisoners and took them apart," Jake said bitterly.

"I shall pretend that I did not hear that wild and careless accusation," the colonel said with pleasure. "And you watch your step, Captain. You can rest assured that I certainly will."

Once they had completed their official business, their return journey was held to a slow, dusty crawl. An endless line of trucks, armored personnel carriers, battle tanks, and heavy-equipment conveyors filled the road. Pierre waited until they had placed several hours between them and Oberkirch before asking Jake, "So who is this Connors, anyway?"

"Connors is a product of what I call the limousine school of war," Jake replied. "He went directly from OCS to a posting in Washington, and weaseled his way up the ladder from behind the safety of a desk."

"There are officers of this caliber in every corps," Pierre replied.

"Yeah, so I've heard. Connors is a special case, though. He's managed to make quite a name for himself. I was amazed at how many people were eager to give me the lowdown on him when I arrived in Germany."

"What brought him over from Washington?"

"Oh, he sort of resigned himself to the fact that Major Connors would never become General Connors unless he accepted an overseas posting. There was a problem, though."

Pierre made the sound of a clucking hen.

"Give the man a cigar," Jake confirmed. "Connors values his own skin above everything else, and his own comfort a close second."

"I can think of several French officers who are close relations of our dear colonel," Pierre mused. "Birds of a feather, you might say."

"With great care and after much deliberation," Jake continued, "Connors selected a posting to the general staff of the Sixth Army. He waited until the Germans looked pretty well whipped, but not to the point where they were ready to roll over and play dead. The staff headquarters was being moved every week or so, as the front rolled on across Belgium and into Germany. Connors figured he wouldn't have much trouble finding a deep, dark hole if the Germans ever tried to attack."

"Something went wrong," Pierre guessed.

Jake nodded. "Connors failed to take into account the command mentality of the Sixth Army's chief, General George Patton. Patton hates these pencil pushers almost as much as I do."

"As *we* do, mon Capitaine," Pierre corrected. "Don't leave me out of this."

"Right. So according to scuttlebutt, what followed then were the six most harrowing months of Connors' life. He survived —"

"Alas," Pierre interjected. "While too many good men went down."

"And he gained his colonel's wings," Jake went on. "But he also gained a reputation among the battle-hardened officers."

"One with the fragrance of sun-ripened Gorgonzola," Pierre suggested.

"Something like that. So instead of being posted

to Nuremberg or Berlin or another of the great centers of post-war activity, Connors found himself relegated to this backwater near the French border."

"Not the place where one might be expected to have the chance to gain a general's star." Pierre shook his head. "What a pity."

"Rumor has it," Jake replied, "that his commanding officer told him he had almost as much chance of making general as the porcupine did of becoming America's favorite house pet."

"A bitter pill," Pierre said.

"So when I arrived in Oberkirch, I found the gallant colonel busy gathering a company of toughs in MP uniforms. Why, nobody could figure out, but there were a lot of ideas floating around. The one I liked best was that the general's straight talk had turned Colonel Connors into a certified loon."

Sally Anders put it more succinctly that evening over dinner. "Connors is a toad," she declared.

Jake feigned shock. "You're speaking of a superior officer."

"A great hairy toad," she insisted.

"Toads don't have hair," Pierre pointed out.

"This one does," she countered.

"Not that much," Jake said.

"And warts," Sally went on. "I bet he even catches flies with his tongue."

They ate together in the Officers' Mess because Sally had refused to dine with either of them alone, although both had invited her. Jake had even asked twice. Her reply was, you make too good a team to have it broken up fighting over a woman.

Pierre said, "I still don't understand why Connors went after you that way."

"All this fuss over a football game," Jake agreed.

"It doesn't have anything to do with the game," Sally replied. "Not directly, anyway."

"I don't understand."

"You gave people something they've been looking for," Sally explained. "A good reason to laugh at Connors. A group of half-starved German POWs beat Connors' prize battalion at their own game, and did it because they used strategy instead of strength. You punctured the balloon of his dignity, Jake. You showed him for the pompous idiot he is. And he hates you for it."

"How do you know Connors so well?" Pierre asked.

"Jake isn't the only one Connors has bulldozed. We've got several here on our staff who are still nursing wounds."

"We have?"

"Anybody who's seen as a threat to Connors' ambitions is given the chopping block as soon as possible." Sally smiled at Jake. "Given the level of your diplomatic skills, soldier, I'm surprised you lasted as long as you did."

"You should have heard Connors today," Pierre said, and related the episode on the HQ front steps.

"That man is a menace in uniform," Sally declared.

"You won't find much argument with us on that point," Jake said.

"I can't believe he'd do such a thing to innocent men," she fumed. "You're going to have to do something, Jake."

He nodded. "I've been thinking about that."

"And watch your step. You're taking care of a lot right now. Don't forget yourself." She lit up. "No, wait; I've got an idea."

"Suddenly there's a dangerous light in your eyes," Jake said anxiously.

Sally leaned conspiratorially across the table. "Do we agree that Connors shouldn't be allowed to get away with this?"

"Sure, but —"

"No buts," she said sharply. "Did you know that the man's in love with his jeep?"

"He is?" Pierre asked.

"Sure," Jake replied. "Everybody who's ever served with Connors knows about that jeep. He keeps it in a special shed just outside the Oberkirch camp. Every day he manages to catch some poor enlisted man doing something wrong, just so he can order him to wash and wax it."

Pierre's eyes widened. "Wax a jeep?"

"It's the truth, I promise," Jake said. "Had these little throw rugs on the floor, made us scrape off our boots before getting in. Crazy."

"Okay, okay," Sally interrupted. "We already know the man's a maniac. Now what I suggest

121

is we hit him where it hurts."

"The question is," Jake countered. "How much is it going to hurt us?"

"Not at all if we're careful." Sally was on her feet. "You two go get into your dirtiest fatigues. Meet me back here in an hour."

"Where are you going?"

"I've got to see a friend in Stores."

Chapter Nine

The next day, Jake tried to still his queasy stomach as he knocked on Colonel Beecham's door. He found some comfort in the greenish, pasty shade of Servais' face. When the muffled voice thundered from within, Jake swallowed once, turned the handle, and entered.

Beecham's weary expression deepened when they came into view. "Not you two," he groaned. "What do you want now?"

"You sent for us, sir," Jake pointed out.

"Impossible. The only reason I'd do that would be to hand you a pair of postings to Antarctica."

"Does that mean we're dismissed, sir?"

"No, you're here, so I might as well get to the bottom of this." He inspected the two men. "What are you doing in dress uniforms?"

"Our fatigues were, ah, stained, sir."

"Well, go over to Stores and draw out some more. I can't have my men marching around looking like a pair of parade-ground heroes." The colonel shuffled through his papers until he found one. "I've got a requisition order from Stores here. Do you know anything about it?"

Jake and Pierre exchanged baffled glances. "We haven't asked for anything, sir."

"Not you directly. It's from some doctor or other. Le'see, he wants syringes, inoculations for everything from typhus to the yellow peril, and enough other stuff to outfit a field hospital." Beecham lowered the page. "Does this have something to do with those kids?"

"I guess it might, sir."

"You guess." Beecham snorted. "Are you trying to steal my doctors, son?"

"Nossir, nothing like that. They just asked if they could help out."

"I'll bet." He studied the paper a moment longer, then scrawled his signature and thrust it forward. "Have Miss Anders try to sell the idea to the local Red Cross. But if they kick up a fuss, tell Stores I said it was okay."

"Yessir. Thank you, sir."

"And Burnes."

"Sir?"

"Don't bother me again. Not today. Not this week. Not for a month or so. Not if you value your hide. It's time for you and your sidekick to vanish from my sight."

"We'll make like the wind, sir," Jake promised.

"That'll be the day," Colonel Beecham said. "Oh, one more thing. Do either of you know anything about how Colonel Connors' jeep received a complimentary paint job last night?"

Jake found it difficult to keep his gaze straight, his voice level. Very difficult. "Nossir."

"Canary yellow, if I understand it correctly."

"News to me, sir."

"The perpetrators apparently attached a feather-duster to the rear bumper." Colonel Beecham found it necessary to frown fiercely over the news. "They painted large chickens in flight on either door. And wrote 'Property of the Chicken Colonel' across the front."

"Can't imagine who would do such a thing," Jake replied.

"Funny," Beecham said in a low voice. "I could come up with several dozen names right off the top of my head. Which is exactly what I told Connors when he called me this morning and accused you two of doing the dirty deed."

To that Jake made no reply.

"All right, make yourselves scarce." Beecham dropped his eyes back to his papers. "Permanently."

Once back in the hallway, Pierre observed, "Our colonel is looking weary."

"Exhausted," Jake replied. "Utterly exhausted."

"We must try not to bother him further," Servais said.

"I'll explain the situation to Sally," Jake offered.

Pierre smiled. "Come, my friend. Let us go and tell her together. I no longer feel I can trust you alone with her."

But it was Sally who found them, a wide-eyed, fearful Sally who ran up and cried breathlessly,

"You've both got to come with me at once."

"What's wrong?"

Sally had already turned on her heel and headed for the door. "There's no time to lose!" she called back. "Hurry!"

She asked them to stop by the hospital for a fourth passenger, Dr. Harry Weaver. The young man came racing down the stairs as soon as the jeep pulled up, black bag in hand. "I'm due in surgery in two hours," he said, climbing on board. "We'll have to hurry."

"Would somebody mind telling me what's going on?" Jake asked.

"To the chocolate factory," Sally cried. "Step on it!"

Pierre was sufficiently caught up in the urgency to throw caution to the winds. Conversation was impossible. All three passengers were kept busy simply trying to stay in the bouncing jeep.

They pulled up in front of the gang's ruined building to find Chaplain Fox waiting by the door. He waved them to a stop, his customary smile gone, his eyes grave with concern. As soon as the doctor alighted, Fox took one arm and led him forward, leaving the others to find their own way.

The stench hit Jake before he was over the entrance plank. The odor was so strong it was a physical shock. He forced himself onward, reached the doorway to the gang's single room, then stopped.

The doctor bent over an inert body. Jake im-

126

mediately recognized Karl, the young leader. The boy moaned softly, struggling to move. He was restrained by the chaplain, who leaned over him, murmuring gently in his ear. Beside Karl, two bodies were stretched out, another boy and a girl. The smell from them, too, was a solid force, so strong it was difficult to breathe in the room.

"What is it?" Jake managed.

"It's just as I feared," the doctor replied, rocking back on his haunches. "We have been receiving reports from other regions, but this is the first confirmed case in this area. It's not surprising, of course. It tends to attack the young, the weak, the unprotected."

"What does," Jake demanded.

The doctor gave a sigh of resignation. "Cholera. Also known as the plague."

Chapter Ten

There was never enough time. There was never enough of anything. Jake moved in a constant, wearying blur, his mind always filled with all that remained undone.

No one assigned him the duty. Jake did not question how or why he shouldered these tasks. He simply did what was required. He had to. It was only later that he wondered at his unquestioning response to a call he had never heard. Not with his mind, anyway.

The first crisis arrived soon after they loaded the four inert youngsters into the jeep, and he and the doctor careened off to the local Red Cross clinic. The chaplain, Sally, and Servais stayed behind, heading off in different directions to do a rapid survey of the other gang hideouts.

Jake and Harry Weaver were met at the hospital by another staunch member of the No Brigade, a large doctor in starched whites. "Just a minute there, Captain," he said sternly as they came rushing up the stairs with Karl and another of the boys in their arms. "Where on earth do you think you're going?"

"This boy needs medical attention," Jake snapped. "There are two more in the same condition out in the jeep. Could you ask two of your staff to give us a hand?"

"Not so fast, not so fast." The doctor moved to block Jake's forward progress. "Where are these kids' papers?"

"They have no papers."

"Then this is out of the question," the doctor insisted. "This clinic is specifically designated to assist the citizens of this town only. And only those citizens whose papers are in order. As it is, my staff and I are stretched to the limit. The absolute limit. You will simply have to cart this boy and his friends off elsewhere."

"Wait," Harry Weaver began. "I am —"

"Hold it, Harry," Jake said, his voice ominously low. "Let me handle this one."

As gently as he could, Jake lowered Karl's limp body to the floor. He then turned, grabbed the clinic doctor by his lapels, lifted him clear off the floor, and in two swift steps slammed him up against the side wall.

"Now look here," the doctor said, his voice up two full octaves.

"No, Doc," Jake snarled back, his face a scarce three inches from the doctor's nose. "You look real good. You search that small mind of yours and make dead certain there's not some other clause you might have missed." He slammed the heavy man back against the wall like an oversized puppet. The doctor let out a high-pitched squeak.

129

"You better *hope* there's something you've forgotten, Doc." Another slam. Another squeak. "That is, unless you'd like me to show you just how thin you can be stretched."

The doctor drew a breath with difficulty and managed to gasp, "Well, now, I think we might be able to do something."

Jake let the man drop, and wiped his hands on his coat. "Four beds," he commanded. "More when we need them. Or I'll be back."

"Really, Captain," the doctor said, collecting himself. "There's no need for threats."

"That was no threat, Doc," Jake replied, stooping down to lift Karl up again. "That was nothing but cold hard fact. Now let's see those beds."

Death became his enemy, shortages his greatest foe. Jake fought with the same single-minded purpose that had brought him and his men through other earlier battles. He fought with all that he had at his disposal, accepting help from whichever quarter it might come. He fought with the desperate determination of a commander who knew that preserving the lives of his men was his most sacred responsibility.

The chaplain, Sally Anders, and Pierre Servais were Jake's chief lieutenants. But there was never any question of who was in charge. There was no time to question it. Nor was there any need. Jake simply shouldered the burden and charged.

The change was mirrored in others. Children who had never learned to obey anyone or anything were gradually coming to follow instructions instantly and to the letter. At least they did so when the commands came from Jake. Pierre, since he spoke no German, became supplies driver and chauffeur extraordinaire.

Chambers that had harbored sick children were swept and scrubbed for the first time since the war's end. Proper latrines were dug. The chaplain took over the rubble heap next door to the crèche; with the help of some of the children he cleared a space, erected a shelter, and started an indoor-outdoor kitchen where the gangs could come and sit on dry ground and eat a decent hot meal at least once a day.

And of course, all of this meant that Jake had to scrounge for even more supplies.

Help began arriving from the strangest sources. Mornings would often begin to the sound of growling truck motors, staffed by men he did not know, coming from bases as far away as Stuttgart and Heilbronn, sent by officers he had never met. Each frantic day he would pass soldiers, speak with them, issue orders, alert them to a new outbreak or a point of urgent need, then hurry on, only to wonder afterward who he had just addressed.

Perhaps the greatest surprise was when the big-bellied, cigar-chewing Sergeant Morrows turned up at Jake's quarters late one evening. "What say, Captain."

"Sergeant." Jake assumed the sergeant was bringing a reprimand from the colonel for having shirked his duties, but he was too tired to care. He scrubbed a fatigue-numbed face with his towel, and slumped down on his bed.

The sergeant scuffed his boots on the doorjamb and said, "Quite a little operation you've got going here."

Jake closed his eyes with a long, deep sigh. The problem with such nights was that while his body begged for sleep, his mind had lost its ability to slow down.

"Me and the boys, well, we've been talking." Morrows seemed to be finding his speech hard going, but he plugged on. "See, the thing is, sir, my specialty in the war was sort of being able to find things."

Jake rolled his head on the pillow and opened one eye.

"Not steal, you understand. Nothing like that. Just sort of find them. And, well, like I said, me and the boys were just talking, and —"

"Disinfectant," Jake said.

"We, ah, what was that, sir?"

"We need disinfectant," Jake repeated. "Urgently. Gallons of it. Enough to scrub down the floors and walls of maybe a hundred rooms."

"Disinfectant. Right." From a pocket the sergeant produced a grubby envelope and a two-inch stub of a pencil. "Twenty gallons ought to do it? How about brushes and buckets?"

"Transport," Jake said wearily to the ceiling. "We're having problems getting the kids to the hospital, and the doctors to the kids, and the kids to the feeding center, and supplies every-where."

"Don't see much problem there," Morrows said, scribbling busily. "One of my buddies runs the mechanics over at the motor pool. Either the commander lets them have some time off or he'll have to try to drive around on four flat tires."

"And drivers," Jake said. "And more strong backs. And building materials. We've got to make these rooms where they're living dry. And warm."

"Blankets and bedding too, right?" Morrows seemed undaunted by the growing list. "How about more clothes?"

"And food," Jake said. "Those kids eat more than a brigade coming out of battle. There's never enough food."

"You leave it with me, Captain. And get your-self some rest. You look done in." Morrows closed the door and stomped off.

Jake closed his eyes, sighed again, and rolled over on his side. Maybe tonight would be dif-ferent.

Just when it appeared that they were almost on top of the most urgent needs, Jake was blindsided once again. And from the most un-expected direction.

He stopped by the kitchen to make certain Chaplain Fox had enough food and fuel for the day, before working through the Matterhorn of paper work accumulating on his desk. But while Jake was talking to the chaplain, a voice behind him said, *"Entschüldigen Sie mir, bitte, Herr Kapitän."*

Jake turned to find a woman wrapped in rags. A young girl stood by her feet, clutching onto her skirt, and peering fearfully up at Jake. Another child was in the woman's arms, a boy of perhaps four or five. Painfully thin. And inert. Jake did not need to look closer. Not anymore. The smell lingering around the boy was all the information he needed.

"You must take him to the Red Cross center," Jake told the woman. "Immediately."

"Please, Herr Kapitän," she said, her eyes brimming with tears. "My name is Friedrichs. I am a poor woman. My husband was a Nazi. SS. They see me and read my papers and they spit on me. But my boy, my only boy, he is sick. He is dying. Please, please, I beg you, a poor weak woman who has nothing and no one. I hear what you do for the children. All the city hears. Please help me, Captain. Save my boy from death."

Jake started to turn to the chaplain, only to be stopped by the most unexpected of sounds. Under his breath, the chaplain was singing. *Singing.* Jake sighed and shook his head. He reached for the boy.

"I will do what I can," Jake told her.

At that the woman broke down completely.

"You and your daughter must stay and eat with us," he said. "And we will try to find some warmer clothes for you." Jake started for the jeep. "And disinfectant for your home. You must take care that you and the other children do not also become ill."

After that, the sad little lines began to form each day long before Jake arrived. The women refused to speak with anyone save the captain. They would relinquish their children to no one but the captain. Jake began to arrive at the feeding station earlier and earlier, knowing that even an hour in the fierce winter weather would be enough to doom the weakest of the children. And still they were there before he arrived.

New squads were formed to hand out clothing, disinfectant, brushes and pails to each family. They came and deposited their precious, stinking bundles and were sent on their way weeping with pathetic thanks. Addresses were recorded. Notices were printed up in German, so that neighbors could be warned. Jake made the signs as official as possible, *ordering* the cowed populace to take no measure against the families with sickness, *ordering* the neighbors to come in for disinfectant and blankets and food, *ordering* them to take every possible measure to keep their families healthy, *ordering* them to report any sign of illness as soon as it appeared.

But despite their best efforts, the cholera spread. Surely not as quickly as it would otherwise have done, maybe not as rapidly as in other regions. But Jake did not afford himself the luxury of a yardstick. All he saw was the growing number of kids sick and on the borderland of death. And some over the border.

Grudgingly, the clinic gave them an entire ward, which they swiftly filled with so many mattresses that doctors and nurses and volunteers had to pick their way between them gingerly. Even so, it was not enough.

Finally, a delegation headed by Jake approached Colonel Beecham. The colonel replied that he could not go against explicit orders and allow civilians into the military hospital, especially those suffering from a highly contagious disease. But he then ordered a pair of heated Quonset huts, formerly used as warehouse space for kitchen perishables, to be given over to the relief effort. In less than a week, both were filled with moaning, crying, wailing, and sometimes dying children.

The extra space was enough. Barely, but enough.

Slowly, so gradually that at first no one was willing to believe it, the tide turned.

The number of incoming children began to drop. Then drop farther still. Then diminish to a trickle. And those in care began to improve — most of them, anyway.

The exhausted worry lines that had creased the faces of those who had given of their time and energy and love began to disappear. Smiles re-emerged. People who had taken part in the effort found themselves bonded together in the joy of shared achievement, of having given without heed to self or selfish gain. Without self-congratulations, they felt a kind of pride. And for some, their efforts brought a healing of their own internal wounds. They could not have said why, nor where it came from. Yet these war-scarred men and women found themselves walking taller, their own burdens somehow lightened. They discovered that by helping the helpless, they too had been gifted the invisible hand of peace.

Even Jake managed a few nights of uninterrupted sleep.

Chapter Eleven

Jake himself decided they might actually have rounded the corner the day he took Karl home.

The boy was sunken-eyed and silent as the jeep wound its way through littered, bomb-pitted streets. But when they pulled up in front of the chocolate factory, Karl announced in German, "I will find what you are seeking."

It took a moment for Jake to realize what Karl was talking about. The last thing on his mind for weeks had been the possibility of unearthing lost Nazi treasure. "Have your team look all you want," Jake replied. "But you concentrate on getting well."

"Yes, I get well, so I can work for you," Karl replied. "But others will not do this work. Me. I work. And not just look. I find."

Jake understood him perfectly. "You don't owe me anything."

"No, nothing at all, just life. Is my life not worth something, Captain?"

Jake found himself admiring the boy's spirit. "You're going to be okay."

As he lifted himself from the jeep, Karl's eyes

burned with renewed determination. He nodded once to Jake. "I find."

That afternoon Jake and Pierre returned to their liaison duties with heavy hearts. After weeks of neglect, they could only expect to find their fledgling border patrols in total disarray. Not to mention the state of their personal contacts with the chain of command.

Yet when they stopped at the main gate of the Karlsruhe base, the guard threw them a parade-ground salute and motioned for the gate to be swung open.

"Captain Burnes and Captain Servais to see Major Hobbs," Jake said, eyeing the open gate.

"Sure, sir. I know you. I brought a truck down your way a couple of weeks ago." The corporal motioned them forward. "You know the way, sir."

"Ah," Jake hesitated. "Maybe you'd better call ahead, soldier. Major Hobbs isn't expecting us."

"No problem, sir," the corporal replied. "I'm sure he'll be happy to see you."

Jake glanced at Pierre, but found only a mirror for his own confusion. He turned back. "You are?"

"Oh, yessir. Matter of fact, the major's started his own project to help the kids around here. I'm involved. It's great being able to do something for them, isn't it, sir?"

"Yes," Jake murmured. "Yes, I suppose it is."

"I'll call the major and let him know you're

on your way, Captain. And thanks. You've been a real inspiration to a lot of us around here. Other bases, too, from the sound of things." He snapped out another salute, and waved them on through.

Once beyond the gate, Jake asked, "Did I hear what I thought I heard?"

Pierre shook his head. "My friend, I shall reserve judgment on that one."

Major Hobbs met them with a wry smile. "Do you have any idea how tough you've made it for guys like me?"

"Sir?"

"Oh, drop the sirs and siddown, both of you." Hobbs settled back in his chair, cranked it back, and propped up his feet. "I mean, if I'm going to be the model to my men that the general's always going on about, I now have to live up to the examples of Captains Jake Burnes and Pierre Servais. Did I get your name right, Captain?"

"Close enough," Pierre said distractedly.

"The general?" Jake asked dully.

"You'd think you two had found the end of the rainbow, the way Command's been going on recently." Despite his words, the major did not appear the least bit put out. "Yeah, Colonel Beecham's report must have really caught their attention."

"Colonel Beecham wrote a report to Command?" Jake asked.

"Hard to believe, I admit. Seeing the pair of you sitting there so dog-tired you can barely talk,

I have trouble understanding what all the hullabaloo is about. But the colonel obviously disagreed. Had some nice things to say about you two. Haven't seen it myself, but from what I hear he really laid it on thick."

"He didn't tell us about any report," Jake said.

"No?"

"Not a word," Pierre confirmed.

Hobbs did not bother to hide his grin. "Probably figured a pair of swollen heads would just get in the way. But there you are. The brass are talking about the little miracle you've worked. Burnes and Servais, those're the words of the month."

"We didn't work any miracle," Jake protested weakly.

"It's not enough that I've got to spend all my free time prying goods loose from Stores, so I can send it down to you guys," Hobbs went on. "Nossir. Now I've got to go out and get my own hands dirty."

"This is the first we've heard about any of this," Jake stammered. "We just came up to find out how the patrols —"

"Oh, that's all taken care of," the major said with a wave of his hand. "I've got two full platoons assigned to it round the clock. Border's not tight as a corked jug, mind you, not by a long shot. But we're bringing in our share of would-be smugglers and refugees. Enough to make you two shine in your own reports."

"That's good news," Pierre said, as stunned

141

as Jake. "Very good."

"Yeah, had to cover you boys while you were out making the world healthy and safe for democracy." The grin broadened. "Interesting how I still don't lack for patrol duty volunteers, seeing as how it's cold as the backside of beyond out there. I guess the treasure hounds are still hungry, even though they haven't come across any pack trains of diamond-studded gold bars or whatever you guys stumbled over."

"A cross," Jake corrected. "Just one cross."

"Just, the man says. Anyway, I got patrol volunteers running outta my ears."

"This is, well . . ." Jake turned to Pierre for help.

"Incredible," Servais finished for him. "We are deeply grateful."

"Glad to hear it." Major Hobbs dropped his feet to the floor with a resounding thump. "Seeing as how you two are now in my debt, I'd like you gents to come give my boys a little pep talk."

"A what?"

"Lay it all out. Describe what needs to be done and how to go about doing it. Cholera's appeared in three districts of this town already. The cellar kids are supposed to be dropping like flies. We heard you got it pretty much licked down your way. Is that right?"

"It appears so," Pierre replied. "But it's too early to tell for sure."

"Well, at this stage we're ready to try anything.

142

So how about you two coming back tomorrow around eighteen-hundred hours, and telling my boys where to start and what to do next."

"I'm not much of a speaker," Jake protested.

The major waved it aside. "We asked for volunteers the day before yesterday, and got more offers than we can handle. They've heard about what you've been doing, I guess from the guys trucking down supplies, and now everybody and his cousin wants to get on the bandwagon. We'll use today to get the word out to be ready in time for your talk tomorrow. Okay?"

"I suppose —"

"Great. Anyway, it'll give you a chance to polish your act before laying it on for the general staff." The major was on his feet, hand outstretched. "Sure is good to know I can count on you guys."

Jake dropped Servais off at the headquarters building in Badenburg and headed toward the center of town. He found Chaplain Fox surrounded by helpers at the feeding station, preparing the day's meal. They had long since found it necessary to declare the lot off limits until the chaplain had blessed the meal and serving had begun; as a result, a crowd was already gathering just outside the lot's perimeters. If he had not been so distracted, Jake would have taken great comfort from the fact that a few of the kids had actually had enough energy to start a game of tag down the street.

Jake pulled the chaplain over to one side and

told him about all the fuss being made over the relief effort. He finished with the complaint, "I'm not a hero. I don't even *feel* like a hero."

"Not many honest people do, Jake."

"What's that supposed to mean?"

"Most heroics are built on tragedy," Chaplain Fox replied. "And most heroes do not act alone. If a man is honest with himself, he can take little pleasure in gaining from someone else's misery. And he will always feel uncomfortable if people make him into a symbol for the noble actions of many."

Jake kicked at a loose stone, sending it spinning across the rubble-strewn lot. "So what is the answer?"

"Allow God to use you for His glory, not for your own," he answered simply. "When your moment of honor comes, remember David's prayer. Who am I, David asks of God, that you would call me by name? And what have I done that causes you to give such greatness to your servant's house?" The chaplain paused to smile at the little girl whose mother was tending the cooking fire, then continued. "Here at the moment when David is being crowned king of all Israel, he humbles himself before God and declares himself a *servant*. That to me is the only sane way to approach recognition and honor. To dedicate it to the Lord and seek to do His will."

Jake was still mulling over the chaplain's words when a voice behind him called out, "Excuse me please, Herr Kapitän."

He turned and saw Frau Friedrichs, the first woman who had brought her sick child to him. The memory of most faces were blurred by hurry and fatigue. But as she had been the first, Jake recognized her immediately. He walked over and asked in German, "How is your son?"

"Weak," she replied, her voice long since drained of all emotion. It was as flat and as hollow as her features. "Very weak. But he lives."

Jake nodded. He had seen too many of the children hanging on by the slenderest of threads. Too many. "Is he taking any food?"

"Your priest gives me what he can," she replied. "I make a soup. He drinks some when he wakes up."

He noted the darkened rings surrounding her sunken eyes, the hollowed cheeks. "Then he should live."

She nodded. "You are a good man. You did all you could."

"Not enough," Jake replied. The wound of seeing so many little bodies buried was with him still. "And your daughter?"

"She is well, thanks to you and your men. And thanks to your orders to clean and disinfect, only one other child in the block was ill. And because of your signs, the neighbors don't scream for us to leave anymore, to get out from our home, when we have no place else to go."

"For this I am glad," Jake replied quietly.

The woman dredged up the faintest hint of a smile. "When one has nothing, even the smallest bit of hope is very big, is that not so, Herr Kapitän?"

Suddenly Jake was struck by the thought that there was an entire city of mothers just like this one in Karlsruhe, all terrified by the thought of their children being snatched away by death. He stepped back, as if physically assaulted by the enormity of the crisis, pressed by the multiplied sorrow and the burden of all the pleas for help.

"Captain?"

In this moment of clarity, Jake no longer saw just this one scarred and exhausted woman. He saw a whole nation in desperate need. He saw all those who extended their hands in the terror of a dark and lonely room, with no one to help, no one to call upon, and knew he had to go. There was no choice. "Yes," he said softly.

"The children," Frau Friedrichs continued. "The children of the street, they tell me you seek Nazi treasure."

Jake focused on her with difficulty. "I am not —"

"I wish to help you, Captain," she went on. "I and many others. Others who have some hope today because of you and your men."

"It is not necessary," Jake protested. "You have enough to do just caring for your family."

"For me, yes, it is necessary." The woman straightened herself with visible effort. "My husband was a Nazi. But he and all he stood for is gone. Gone. Gone to the graveyard of tragic error. It is finished, thank God. It is finished."

"Yes," Jake agreed, and could only admire her strength.

"He never spoke of treasure. But I know of others who heard things. I will ask. I will search papers. And whatever I find is yours."

"Thank you," Jake said solemnly. "You shall receive your share of whatever is brought to me."

The news brought the faintest glimmer to her weary eyes. "Perhaps I should refuse, but I cannot. I shall accept anything you give, but not for me."

"For your children," Jake said, nodding. "I understand."

"You should know something, Captain," the woman continued. "Others are searching."

"I have heard."

"Men with white helmets and white sticks," she told him. "Men who have evil eyes and voices."

The news rocked him. "Connors?" he asked of no one in particular.

"They do not offer anything in return," she went on. "They do not bring kindness. They come in danger, and they wreak havoc. If they are against you, Herr Kapitän, then you must take care. Great care. I fear they are friends to no one but themselves."

Sally found him wandering around headquarters a few hours later. "You look lost, soldier."

"I was looking for Pierre. Sort of, anyway."

She searched his face, said, "What's wrong, Jake?"

He looked around to make sure no one else was within range, then said quietly, "I just had an indication that Connors might be hunting for Nazi treasure."

"So?"

"You don't find that surprising?"

"If you hang around these halls long enough, you'll be surprised at the things you can pick up." A group of officers exited noisily from a conference room. Sally grasped his arm and steered him away. "You've got to admit it makes sense."

"What does?"

"Come on, Jake. Connors may be a hazard, but he's no fool."

"He's not?"

"No, he isn't, and you know it. He probably had some treasure-hunting scheme festering in that little mind of his when he started collecting that gang of hooligans."

"It makes sense," he said slowly.

"Sure it does. You stick with Sally, soldier. She'll take care of you."

"But I never figured Connors for a money-grubber."

"Connors likes his own comfort, but I doubt that money is behind all this activity. What Connors wants most is power." She popped into her office and came out shrugging on her coat. "I've been cooped up in here all day. Mind taking

148

a lady for a walk?"

"Not at all."

"There's a general in Freiburg who's gained a reputation for wanting to crown his career by unearthing a major Nazi hoard," Sally continued. "It's my guess that Connors has linked up with him, in return for a promise of those little stars for his shoulder pads."

Jake pushed through the door, returned the guard's salute, and declared to Sally, "The day Connors gets his promotion is the day I hang up my hat."

"You and me both, soldier. But for the next fifteen minutes, let's pretend Connors and all the rest don't exist, okay? I mean, a weary woman can take only so much of the world."

"Fine with me," Jake said, turning with her to follow the road away from town.

They walked in silence for a time, passing through a growth of tall trees before emerging into a pasture-like clearing. Sally took a breath. "Back home, this is what we'd call a big sky," she said, her face suddenly open and relaxed, her skin lit by the day's waning light.

Clouds scuttled high overhead and down along the horizon, cloaking a winterland scene back-lit by the late afternoon sun. "Sure is a good day to be alive," Jake said.

"And healthy," she added. Then more quietly, "I've missed you, Jake."

"I've missed *you* — very much."

"You've been too busy to miss anybody."

"Not you," he replied. "Not ever."

Her look softened. "I'm proud of what you did. Very, very proud."

"I'm not sure who it was behind the doing," he confessed.

"What's that supposed to mean?"

Jake struggled for a moment, wanting to share his thoughts, but not sure he could, even with himself. "It just didn't make any sense."

"It made all the sense in the world," Sally corrected.

"Wait, let me try to explain. Logically, I mean. None of this was any of my business." He stopped and turned toward her. "But I've never felt so sure of anything in my whole life, Sally. Can you make any sense out of that?"

She looked up at him. "And you said you weren't a believing man."

"I'm not." He stopped, then admitted, "Or at least I wasn't. I'm not so sure about anything anymore. And the chaplain said some things to me this afternoon that . . ."

Sally nodded slowly. "I know," she assured him. "That man has a way of making it all seem so clear. So *possible*."

"What he's suggesting suddenly seems the most sensible thing in the whole world," Jake agreed.

"Who knows," she said, taking his arm. "Maybe it is, and we're just slow to find out."

Chapter Twelve

"I'll flip you for it," Jake offered as they entered the Karlsruhe base the following evening.

"No need, my friend," Pierre replied. "You have already been volunteered."

"This is worse than going into battle," Jake groaned.

Pierre nodded. "I agree. In battle all they do is shoot you. There is no telling what the high command will do if you mess this one up."

Jake glared at his friend. "Thanks a lot."

"Something slow, I would imagine," Pierre suggested. "Undoubtedly very painful."

Jake pointed to where Major Hobbs was motioning them over. "I think he means us."

"I happen to have a blindfold in my pocket if you think it would help," Pierre offered, and wheeled the jeep into place.

"Glad to see you boys," the major said in greeting. "We've got quite a crowd in there."

Jake gave a soft moan.

"Something wrong with our man?"

"A touch of indigestion," Pierre assured him. "Nothing serious."

"Oh. Right. Okay, here's the plan. I'll stand up and make just a couple of remarks — you know, pave the way for the main action. Then I'll introduce you, and you get on with the show."

Jake wiped clammy hands down his pantlegs.

"We've talked it over," the major continued. "And we don't think there's any need for you to go into great detail. We can handle that ourselves. What we need from you is a little pep talk, something to inspire them to get out there and work."

"That's what Jake is best at," Pierre offered. "Inspiration."

"Great, just great. Exactly what I wanted to hear." The major clapped Jake on the shoulder. "Okay, let's get this show on the road."

The several hundred men and women crowded together transformed the hall into a smoky din. Jake shook hands with a variety of officers, nodded greetings, stood while introductions were being made, yet heard not a word of what was said. Someone led him up onto the stage and directed him into a rickety folding chair. Jake sat and watched as the major approached the podium and called for order. He half listened as the major entertained the group with a few jokes. Then the major turned and pointed toward him. Applause swept through the hall. Jake knew it was time.

He found it to be just like the moment before combat. As soon as it started, his nerves quieted down. Jake stood and walked forward to the podium, shook the major's hand, waited for the applause to die. And somehow he knew what he needed to say. The words had long been there, just waiting for an opportunity like this to be spoken.

"You will all find your own reasons for doing this," Jake began. "Or you will quit. There is no glory in this work. There aren't any medals. Nobody is waiting to pat you on the back and say what a great job you have done. And what you are going to find when you get out there is not pretty. As a matter of fact, it is about as ugly and disgusting as it comes. So if you are not able to find something in yourselves to keep you going, you'd better get out. All I can tell you is what worked for me."

A hush gathered, a stillness from a deeper place of listening and understanding. The room became so quiet Jake could hear the occasional foot sliding across the polished floor. "Anyone of you who has been in combat knows what it is like to take a village, or a hill, or a river, or whatever the objective might be. When it's over, you're bone-tired, more exhausted than you ever thought possible. Maybe you just saw a couple of your friends take a hit. Maybe you came close enough yourself to death to still have the feel of it lingering around you. So there you are. You sprawl out, maybe grab a quiet smoke and a cup of java. And what happens? Out of nowhere comes this cluster of little kids.

"Your first reaction is, go away. But you're

153

probably too dog-tired even to say the words. So the kids hang around, just out of reach, and they stare at you. All rags and dirt and limbs as thin as little sticks."

Here and there in the room, heads began nodding as Jake intoned scenes and memories. "Then you move on," Jake continued. "It's strange what you remember from all that just happened. After coming that close to death, you'd expect the most vivid recollections to be of the battle. But that is not the way it works, at least not for me. No, what I remember most clearly is how big those kids' eyes looked. I used to think that all the war and suffering they had seen somehow opened their eyes to twice their normal size." Jake shook his head. "All I have to do is close my own eyes, and their faces are still there, still staring back at me.

"So what happens now? We won the war, right? We will be going home soon, at least most of us will. I am, and let me tell you, I am counting the days." Jake waited through the quiet chuckles, then said, "But those faces are still with me, just as I described them. All those kids, in every place I left behind.

"When this problem surfaced down in the town by my own base, I decided that maybe it would be a good idea if I could try to do a little something for just *one* kid. In just *one* town — before I went away and left all the ruin and destruction behind me. Before it was too late."

He stopped and waited for a moment, then

finished, "I know those faces will still be with me until the day I die. But at least now, right there alongside them, will be these other faces. Some with smiles, even. Faces of a few people who might have a little more chance to make something of their lives because of what some of us did, or tried to do. And that is what is most important — that we *tried*. We tried to give them back a little hope."

Chapter Thirteen

When the base at Offenburg asked him to come down and give the same talk two nights later, Jake was less bothered. At least, until Sally Anders insisted on coming along.

"No how, no way," he declared, and tried to turn away.

But Sally was not having it. "You may consider it an order, soldier. You are taking me along, and that's final."

"Over my dead body."

"That can be arranged," she snapped. "Jake, who brought you to meet the kids in the first place?"

"I forget."

"Well, you best just unforget, mister. I'm calling in my chips."

"The only way I get through this is because I'm talking to a bunch of strangers," he pleaded.

"Then you can just consider me one of them," she retorted. "That should be easy enough, as scarce as you've been these past few weeks."

"Sally, you know how overwhelmed I —"

"So here's your perfect opportunity to make

up for lost time." She batted her eyelashes. "Look at it this way. How often does an attractive girl throw herself at you?"

In the end it was all right. Once up on the podium, Jake had no room to think of anything else. The pressure to tell what was in his heart was just too strong.

Afterward, Sally waited while the commanding officers gathered and shook his hand and offered compliments. Her gaze never left his face, not even when Pierre tried to capture her attention. For that moment, that hour, she was his.

Without asking, Jake ushered Sally into the backseat of the jeep, clambered in beside her, then said to Servais, "Home, James."

Pierre surveyed the pair, his eyes dark and unreadable. Then he said, "I suppose it is time for the white flag."

"Don't be silly," she told him, but her voice lacked conviction, and her eyes were still on Jake. "I sat up front with you for the trip here. Turn about is fair play."

Pierre nodded, his expression blank. "Your mouth says one thing," he replied, "your eyes another, ma chérie." Then before Sally could respond, he gunned the motor and started off.

They sped back under a star-streaked sky. The trees were dark guardians lining the road; their sharp spears jutted upward, granting a sense of safety to the surrounding night. Sally shifted from time to time, drawing closer to Jake. Jake took heady draughts of the biting air, and felt that

157

here, this moment, his life might truly begin anew.

Pierre drove with a chauffeur's precision, his eyes ever forward. He spoke not a word. Jake resisted the urge to reach out and pat Pierre's shoulder and offer words of friendship. Now was a time for Sally. She leaned against his chest, she filled his world.

Then they rounded the final corner before entering the city's outskirts, and the peace was shattered.

It was not a full-control checkpoint. Just a trio of whitestreaked MP jeeps set at point, with a series of striped barrels rolled in front and their tops set alight. Spread out around the barrels were a dozen or more white-helmeted soldiers.

"Hang on!" Pierre shouted, simultaneously hitting the brakes and spinning the wheel violently.

The jeep almost went over. It careened up on two wheels, teetered, then slammed back and did a grandiose four-wheel skid into the right-hand pair of barrels. They missed the MPs stationed there only because the men flung themselves out of harm's way.

While Jake was still frozen in the protective position he had taken across Sally, Pierre jumped from the seat. "Come on, move it, move it!"

Jake's muscles obeyed the urgency in Pierre's voice. He lifted a visibly shaken Sally up and out of the jeep. Before her feet were even in contact with the earth, Pierre grabbed her and sped toward the closest shadows. Jake was immediately after them.

The MPs' stunned stillness was shattered by a violent, "After them!"

Tree limbs whipped Jake's face and snatched at his uniform, as if trying to hold him until the assailants could catch up. He fought with an animal's panic strength, struggling to keep up with the racing Servais.

"Through the trees! Over here!"

Thundering feet crashed through the brush behind them, adding speed to their flight. Sally's breath was a series of high-pitched gasps. Jake barely missed slamming into a tree he saw only at the last possible moment. Then came the unmistakable crackling sound of gunfire. Jake dropped, rolled, was up and running again, even before the sound had finished its echoing refrain.

Pierre jinked and weaved, crossed over a rutted track, and slid down the embankment on the other side, dragging Sally after him. Jake followed close on their heels, his breath a thunder in his ears. Pierre struggled up a rise; Jake moved in to take Sally's other arm and help lift her up the steep hillock.

At the top there was danger — a clearing without cover. From the other side, figures bounded out of the shadows, struggling through the high snow toward them. Jake was baffled. Panting hard, he dropped to his knees beside Pierre, wondering how their pursuers could have made it up and around them so fast. No, that wasn't possible, he could still hear the shouts and curses following them through the woods behind. Then who —

"Halt!" A voice carried strong and clear across the snow-covered pasture. "Who goes there?"

Behind them the other voices cut off as though sliced with a knife, and Jake knew a blessed rush of relief. "Captains Burnes and Servais. Who are you?"

"Captain Burnes? Is that really you, sir?" A shadow approached at a run; the moonlight revealed the fresh-faced squad leader from one of their own incoming border patrols. "Captain Servais? And who — Miss Anders? What are you folks doing out here?"

"Do us a favor, Corporal," Servais said, his breath coming in quick snatches. "Walk us back to the main road, will you?"

All three of them were shaky on their feet as they trekked back toward civilization, Sally most of all. She had been trying to run in low-heeled pumps. Jake and Pierre were not much better off, their dress shoes hardly made for open-field running over snow and ice. The soldiers were solicitous, and accepted their account of an attack by a band of raiders with genuine alarm.

When they reached the edge of the road, the corporal motioned to them to stay back, as they were weaponless. He and two of his men crept forward and disappeared. A few moments later they returned. "Looks like they scampered, sir."

Jake and the others emerged onto the road to find only their jeep still remaining. The corporal walked over to it and whistled softly. "Come take a look at this, sir."

160

They had not been satisfied to slash all four tires. The windshield and headlights were shattered. The seats had been hacked to ribbons with a sharp-bladed knife.

"Never seen anything like this," the corporal said. "Crazy how they'd destroy something as valuable as a jeep and not take it off as loot."

"The whole thing's crazy," Jake muttered.

"You can say that again, sir. Never heard of a band attacking military personnel before. Well, maybe we ought to walk you folks on back to the base. Somebody from the motor pool can come get your jeep. Sure doesn't look like it's moving from here on its own steam."

They gathered in Sally's office once the squad had been thanked and sent off. Sally vanished and reappeared with blankets and steaming mugs of coffee. They sat and sipped in silence for a few moments before Jake asked Pierre, "Why did you run?"

"It was automatic," he said succinctly. "I didn't think about it."

"Smart, all the same."

Pierre nodded. "A roving band of Connors' goons sets up a roadblock on the only highway leading back from Offenburg, five hours after curfew. What does that tell you?"

"But it doesn't prove anything," Sally protested.

"No," Pierre conceded. "Not that alone."

"What else is there?"

161

"The fact that they weren't there when we returned," Jake replied. "If it had been a legitimate checkpoint, they would have stayed around to arrest us. They had ample reason after Pierre gave them another sample of his driving skills."

Pierre looked up from his two-handed grip on the mug. "What were they after? That is what I cannot understand."

"The jeep?" Sally offered. "Do you think Connors is still carrying a grudge about that, even when he doesn't know for sure it was us?"

"He knows," Jake countered. "He may lack the proof, but he knows all the same."

"Maybe, but I do not think so," Pierre replied. "Something in my gut says the man would not go to all this trouble over one jeep."

"But what else could it be?" Jake demanded. "What could a couple of border liaison officers have that would rile a man like that?"

They sought the answers in silence, sipping the potent brew and gathering strength from the companionship for quite a while. Finally Sally set down her mug, stood, and rubbed a sore back. "Well, soldiers, this woman is off to bed."

Jake was instantly on his feet. "I'll walk you back."

"No need, but thank you." She smiled at Pierre. "Good night, gallant driver."

"Bonne nuit," he murmured, his eyes on his friend. "Sleep well."

"I intend to." She allowed Jake to follow her down the hall, but at the back door leading to the staff's sleeping quarters, she stopped him with a firm, "It's been great, Jake. Thank you for letting me come along."

He inspected her face and said quietly, "That's it?"

"The trip to dreamland was captivating," she admitted. "But I had a rude awakening to reality on the road home."

"That wasn't reality, Sally," Jake protested. "This is."

For once, her sharp wit deserted her. She dropped her eyes and sighed, "If only . . ."

"If only what," he pressed.

She raised her gaze and said flatly, "Nothing, soldier."

"If you don't tell me, how am I supposed to know?"

"Maybe you aren't," she replied, more gently this time. "Good-night, Jake. Go get some sleep."

Chapter Fourteen

Jake rose the next morning wrapped in the mantle of gloom he had carried to bed the night before. He grunted his responses to Pierre's chatter, and pondered over the pain in his heart. While shaving he gave his face a careful scrutiny, trying to view it as Sally might. What he saw did not leave him reassured.

His face had been hardened by war. There were a few lines, mostly around the eyes and mouth. But not many, not enough to define his features. No, the war had *hardened* him. His chin was drawn like a hatchet, his nose a blade that split his face. The old parting he used to have in his hair was gone; instead, he drew the hair straight back, accenting the aggressive thrust to his jaw. His eyes were direct and cautious. And hard. Hard as the rest of him.

Jake sighed, wiped off the remaining lather, and turned away. A face only a mother could love.

They arrived at staff headquarters just as Sally came tripping down the stairs, half in and half out of her coat. At the sight of her, Jake's heart

164

sped, and his mind sought frantically for something, anything, to change the way things were.

But Sally barely noticed him. She clambered over Jake and spilled into the jeep's backseat, yelling out, "To the hospital! Hurry!"

Jake hung on for dear life as Pierre raced back out the entrance drive and up toward a nearby farmhouse which was now doing duty as the military clinic. He risked a backward glance and asked, "What's going on?"

"They've got him," she said, but quickly interrupted herself to pound on Pierre's shoulder. "Stop!" She pointed to a running figure.

Harry Weaver was racing down the road toward them, looking as harried as Sally and just as grim. He leapt into the backseat. "Have you heard anything more?"

"No," Sally replied.

"About what?" Jake asked.

"Who's got whom?" Pierre demanded.

"Just go!" Sally yelled.

"Where?" Jake and Pierre managed in one voice.

"The stockade!" Sally almost lost control at that point, but with an effort drew herself back from the edge. "They've locked up Buddy Fox. And they hurt him!"

Pierre required no further goading. Jake doubted seriously whether all four tires ever hit the road simultaneously from that point on until they halted before the garrison's makeshift prison.

The stockade occupied the lower portion of

what had once been a bank — the only section still intact after a bomb had done away with the upper four floors as neatly as a barber giving a crew cut. The gaping holes where once tall windows had stood were now sectioned off with cross-iron bars over their lower halves and boards closing off the tops.

A squad of MPs with white batons at the ready were gathered in front of the building. At the front and center stood the same sergeant who had led the checkpoint guard patrol.

Sally did not wait for Jake to alight. As the jeep rolled to a stop, she jumped out and stomped over, ready to do battle once more.

"Let him out," she snapped.

"Can't do that, Miss Anders," the sergeant replied, his eyes on Jake. "Orders."

"You want orders? Okay. Fine." She drew a letter from her pocket, whipped it open, thrust it in the MP's face. "I assume you can read."

The MP shifted his baton, thrusting it under his left arm, and accepted the paper. He kept his eyes on Jake. "How you doing there, Captain?"

"Morning, Sergeant," Jake replied. "How's the nose?"

The sergeant flushed and dropped his eyes to the paper, holding the moment as long as he could.

"Well?" Sally snapped.

"Yeah," the sergeant drawled. "That chaplain created a disturbance downtown. Had this mob crawling all over everywhere. You wouldn't expect a chaplain to incite a riot like that, now, would you?"

"Is that what you call trying to feed starving kids, inciting a riot?" Jake asked.

The sergeant's cold gaze rose back to meet Jake's. "Couldn't hardly get down the street, there were so many people. You know there's an ordinance against gatherings of more than half a dozen Krauts in one place without a permit. You *should* anyway. You being a liaison officer and all."

"That paper in your hand," Sally said, almost dancing with rage, "says that the chaplain has express permission to carry on his work, whatever it might require. It also states that you are ordered to release Chaplain Fox to my custody *immediately*. It is signed by Colonel Beecham, commanding officer of this garrison."

"Shame the chaplain had to go and put up such a fuss when we tried to arrest him," the sergeant went on. "Guess it's like Colonel Connors said. He's been hanging around people who've been a bad influence on him."

"Just get the man," Jake ordered.

"Go spring the chaplain, Jenkins," the sergeant said to one of his men.

"Sure, Sarge."

The sergeant's gaze never shifted from Jake. "Heard you had a little trouble with your jeep the other night, Captain."

"Nothing serious," Jake replied, his voice carrying a cutting edge. "Just a bunch of local roughs.

167

You know the type. Cowards that cut and run at the first sight of a real fight."

Fury blazed in the sergeant's eyes, but before he could respond Jenkins came back through the door. He supported a battered Chaplain Fox by one arm. Sally gasped and raced up the stairs with Dr. Weaver.

She put her arms around the chaplain. "Can you make it down the steps?"

"They destroyed my kitchen," the chaplain moaned, allowing her and the doctor to take almost all his weight. "They tore it all apart and stole all my supplies."

"Must be talking about that mob," the sergeant said. "Didn't hardly have enough men to keep order down there."

"Here, Doc," the soldier said. "Lemmee give you a hand."

"You keep your filthy mitts to yourself," she snapped. "Come on, Buddy. It's all over."

"Not yet, it ain't," the sergeant said. "But it soon will be."

Jake helped them settle the chaplain into the passenger's seat. When everyone else was in, he jumped on the running board. "Let's go."

As they drove away, the sergeant waved his baton in the air and called, "Y'all come back now, y'hear?"

"I just don't understand it," the chaplain mumbled through bruised and swollen lips. "What reason could they possibly have for attacking me?"

"Scum like that don't need a reason," Sally said, wrapping a bandage around his forehead.

"Yes, they do," Jake said.

"Now just raise up your other arm," Harry Weaver said, and pressed down on his chest. "Does that hurt?"

"No, ah, there. Yes, there."

"Okay, can you take a breath for me?" He fitted the stethoscope back into his ears, listened carefully, and said, "Again."

Dr. Weaver dropped the instrument back down around his neck. "All right, you can lower your arm." He took a step back. "I'm afraid you have two cracked ribs. But your jaw is not broken as I first thought, and although there are a number of visible contusions, there is no sign of internal injury."

"Thank you, my dear," Chaplain Fox said to Sally as she tucked in the loose end of the bandage. Then to the doctor, "What does all that mean?"

"You should get better fairly quickly," he replied. "And should require no further treatment, except that I'd like to strap those ribs. And see you again in a few days, just to check your progress."

"So when can I go back to work?"

"In a few days. A week at the outside. That is, if you promise to take it easy and let these ribs heal properly."

"I'm not so sure going back there is such a good idea," Jake said slowly.

"Close the feeding station?" Sally was shocked.

"Give in to those animals? What on earth for?"

"That's just it," Jake complained. "I can't figure out what this is all about. And whatever you think, Sally, this was done for a reason."

"I agree," Pierre said, speaking up for the first time since they had left the stockade. "And I don't think it was the chaplain they were after."

"But the children," Chaplain Fox protested to Dr. Weaver. "If I can't, who will look after the children?"

Sally kept her gaze on Pierre. "So who was it they wanted?"

"Your friend and mine," Pierre replied, "Captain Burnes."

"Me?"

"You."

"But why?" Sally demanded.

"I've been thinking about that," Pierre replied. "And I think I might have an answer. Might, you understand. This is just a guess."

"Sally, my dear," the chaplain began, but was shushed by her gentle pressure on his shoulder.

Sally said to Pierre, "Go on."

"Consider their attack the other night," Pierre said. "We assumed it was revenge for Connors' jeep."

Harry Weaver produced his first smile of the day. "That was you guys?"

Sally ignored him. "So what else could it have been?"

"The next time you plan something like that,"

170

Harry Weaver persisted, "be sure and count me in."

"Something else took place at the same time," Pierre went on. "Something Jake happened to mention in passing, which neither of us thought very important. He talked with a young man of the streets, and also with the widow of a former SS officer. And both promised to help Jake in his quest."

"The treasure?" Jake looked astonished. "But you and I both know we're looking for a needle in a haystack the size of a city."

"Not so fast," Pierre said.

"Even if there was any real chance, that rag-tag bunch don't have a hope of finding it. They've hardly got the strength to tie their own shoelaces, much less hunt for hidden treasure." Jake shook his head. "We don't even know if it really exists. Maybe it's all a myth."

"Let him finish, Jake," Sally ordered.

"Not a myth," Pierre countered. "Not all of it. We have a cross to prove that."

"Or at least the army has," Jake muttered.

"Jake," Sally snapped.

"What if there *were* a treasure," Pierre persevered. "What if our charming friend Colonel Connors knew it existed in this area, and thought he was closing in on it?"

"Then all of a sudden up pops Jake, with this crowd of Germans all throwing up dust and covering the same terrain," Sally added. "People Connors has no control over, people who wouldn't

171

give him the time of day. The man would throw a size-twelve fit."

"And go after the ringleader with a vengeance," Pierre agreed.

Jake looked from one to the other, then declared, "You two are out of your tiny minds."

"Then come up with something better," Pierre challenged.

"Strike that," Sally said, rising from the bedside. "It's time to have a chat with Colonel Beecham."

"You can't bring the colonel in on something like this," Jake protested.

"You just watch me, soldier." Sally pointed toward the chaplain. "Take a good look at what those beasts did to Buddy, then tell me what I can and can't do."

"But we don't know anything for sure."

"We know enough," Sally replied. "Now, are you two coming, or do I have to go in there alone?"

"We're coming," Servais said, standing.

"Pierre," Jake moaned.

"Get up, Jake."

"But the colonel, you heard —"

"On your feet, soldier," Sally ordered.

"Wait," Chaplain Fox called out.

Sally turned back to the bed and said gently, "I'll go and see to your children, I promise. Each and every day."

"I know you will, Sally. And I am eternally grateful." He painfully raised himself up on one

172

arm and said to Jake and Pierre with all the force he could muster, "No violence. If you resort to their tactics, then they have won. No matter what the outcome, they have won."

When Beecham heard what had happened to the chaplain, his jaw clamped and his eyes flashed. He remained stern throughout Pierre's account of their trouble at the crossroads and his subsequent guesswork. Jake sat squirming, convinced that once Pierre had finished, the colonel would extract the truth about Connors' jeep.

Instead, Beecham said, "Some rumors have been drifting around that back you up."

Sally sat up straighter. "What have you heard?"

"What I'm about to tell you is strictly off the record, do you understand?"

The three of them nodded.

Beecham focused on Jake. "Do you remember what I once told you about the general-turned-treasure-hound?"

"Yessir. Isn't he posted somewhere around Freiburg?"

"That's the one. Name's Slade. Up for retirement soon. Word has it that he wants to ride out of here in a blaze of glory."

"And Connors is his man," Sally finished for him. "Just as we thought."

"That's not certain," Beecham warned. "But what I can confirm is that Connors now has some hefty protection. Slade has taken Connors under his wing and given him a free hand to do pretty much as he pleases. I called Slade's office as soon as I heard about this set-to with you folks the other night, and got the brush-off from some snot-nosed Ivy League lieutenant." Beecham was obviously still burning at the memory of this encounter. "Last night I also heard that Slade is trying to get his authority extended to cover this area."

"That means the treasure must be located around here!"

"It means that Slade *might* think something *might* be in these parts," Beecham corrected. "If there really is any, which I'm still not certain about."

"What about the cross?" Sally countered.

"One cross is one cross, not a mountain of gold. But yes, I'm willing to admit that there is at least a chance you are right."

"A big chance," Sally said triumphantly.

"A *dangerous* one," Beecham amended. "If there really is a hunt going on around here, and Connors and Slade both know they're racing against the clock, you can bet your life they'll deal savagely with any ground-level opposition." He glanced at his calendar and went on. "The handover to the French is scheduled for early next month. After that, this will be French-controlled territory, and anything they find will be as far out of Slade's reach as the dark side of the moon."

"So do we tell the kids to hold off the search?" Jake asked.

"You can't do that," Sally protested. "What

174

if Connors does find something?"

"He might anyway," Jake pointed out. "He's got a big organization behind him."

"But you've got contacts closer to the ground," Sally argued.

"You've seen Connors' tactics," Jake replied. "How would you feel if somebody was seriously hurt?"

"The kids will just have to be very careful," Sally said. "And they will. Because you're going to keep an eye on them."

"I think she's right," Colonel Beecham said. "As long as they proceed with extreme caution, I think it should be all right to let them see what they can find. I would hate like the dickens for Connors to end up with a lever to elevate himself to general."

"So would I," Jake agreed.

"Talk to them, Captain," Beecham directed. "If they understand the danger and agree to go ahead carefully, good. If not, call it off. It's your shot either way."

Once they had been dismissed, Jake headed straight for the exit. Sally caught up with him. "Where are you going?"

"I want to see if there's anything around the feeding station that can be salvaged."

"Wait, I'm coming with you. I need to check on the crèche."

"Not so fast," Pierre said. "None of us should go anywhere alone. If any one of us needs to go somewhere, we take an escort. Extreme caution starts with us."

"Agreed," Sally said.

"That's fine with me," Jake murmured, his eyes on Sally.

"All right, then. Let's go."

When they pulled up in front of the crèche, a great crowd of youngsters was milling about the street in front of the feeding station. Jake climbed from the jeep and said glumly, "I guess I'd better go break the news."

"Maybe we can work out something by tomorrow," Sally said hopefully. "A cold meal or something."

Pierre stood on the jeep's running board and searched the crowd. "What are those soldiers doing over there?"

"And those trucks," Sally added, pointing to a pair of green canvas tops beyond the gathering.

Just then a voice bellowed out, "All right, all right! Nobody gets nothing until we see some order around here. Corporal!"

"Yeah, Sarge?"

"You and a coupla men line these jokers up."

"I thought you told me to keep a lookout for the creeps in white hats."

"So line 'em up and keep looking. What are you, some kinda moron?"

"No, but I don't speak the lingo."

"Then, use your hands. They got eyes, don't they?"

Jake looked at a wide-eyed Sally. "What's going on?"

"Isn't that Sergeant Morrows?" she asked him.

"Food," Pierre announced, sniffing the wind. "Somebody is definitely cooking something."

They plowed through the mob, crossed the rubble heap, and came upon a sweating Sergeant Morrows with three frantic helpers. When the sergeant saw them he straightened and said, "Say, it's about time — I mean, glad you could get here, sirs. Hey, Miss Anders. Sure could use some help with these kids."

"What's going on here, Sergeant?"

"We heard what they did to the chaplain, sir. Me and some of the boys, we decided we couldn't let the kids go hungry."

One of the soldiers helping Morrows asked, "How's the chaplain, sir?"

"Dr. Weaver says he's going to be okay," Jake replied. He pointed at the gleaming new kettles and stands, the heaps of produce, the shiny steel platters and other equipment and asked, "Where did all this come from?"

"Turned out Stores had some stuff lying around they didn't need." Morrows caught the glint in Jake's eye and protested, "It ain't stolen, sir. Honest. Everybody's real hot over what they done to the chaplain."

"Sarge was turning stuff away," his assistant offered. "Volunteers too. Everybody wanted to get in on the act."

"Put a dozen or so guys spread out in front and back, in case the goons show up again," Morrows said. "I sorta hope they do."

Pierre put up a warning finger. "No violence, the chaplain said."

"There ain't gonna be no violence unless they come looking for it," Morrows replied. "And if they do, it won't last long. Sir."

"Why do you think they did it?" Sally probed.

"Goons is goons, ma'am," Morrows replied. "That's all the reason they need."

Sally nodded her satisfaction to Jake and said, "Looks like everything is under control here, soldier. I'll be in the crèche if you need me."

"I'll help out here," Pierre said to Jake. "Now would be a good time for you to spread the word."

Jake nodded, turned to Morrows, and said something he had never imagined he could say to this man. "You're a good friend, Morrows. To me and to the kids."

"Shoot, sir," Morrows replied, reddening. "It's a pleasure. Never knew anything so easy could mean so much."

Chapter Fifteen

By the next day, word had spread through the garrison that the MPs who raided the feeding station had actually been after Jake and Pierre. Reinforcements had poured in. A guard routine had been set up for both the feeding station and the crèche. At Sally's insistence, another jeep had been requisitioned from motor pool, and a pair of brawny PFCs followed Jake and Pierre wherever they went.

When they stopped in front of the crèche that afternoon on their way to a meeting in Freudenstadt, Pierre told him, "You go ahead, my friend. I'll wait out here."

"What is this?"

Pierre shrugged. "Only a fool continues fighting after the battle is lost. Sally has chosen the victor."

"If she has," Jake declared, "she hasn't told me about it."

"Give her time," Pierre said. "If either of us stands a chance, it's you."

Jake walked down the stairs and pushed through the crèche door. Sally was kneeling in a corner of the room, so involved with a trio of young

179

girls that she did not notice his arrival.

On her face was the same look of unguarded tenderness she had had when speaking of her dead fiance. A flame rose unbidden within Jake, one so strong it threatened to turn his heart to cinders. There was no defense against this fire. Nowhere to run, no way to escape, not without pushing this woman from his life entirely. And that he could not do. Not even with logic whispering endlessly in his mind, she is not for you, not for you, not for you.

Jake watched her, wanted her, and wondered if there was even a chance, the slenderest of threads, that he might take the place of a man who was no more.

He feared her answer as he feared the pain of having her catch sight of him, and watching the tender expression disappear. As quietly as he could, Jake started back out the door.

"Jake?"

Reluctantly he turned back. Sally was already standing and walking forward, smiling and happy to see him. At the sight of her shining eyes, he felt as if a knife were being turned in his stomach.

"Are you off for your talk?" she asked. "Where do you have to go?"

"Freudenstadt."

"I wish I could hear you speak again," she said with real feeling. "But three of the kids are not well, and Harry promised to stop by later."

"I understand," he said quietly.

180

She searched his face. "What's the matter, Jake?"

The simple fact of her calling him by his name was almost too much to bear. He inspected the ground at his feet and said softly, "I have to go."

She didn't answer. Her silence lifted his gaze. He found her watching him with the stillness of a frightened forest creature. Jake did not stop to think, or wonder, or hope. His desire was too great.

He bent and kissed her.

A chorus of high-pitched giggles separated them. Sally managed a shaky smile. "We've got company."

Jake nodded, not trusting his voice just then. He caressed her cheek, then turned and left the crèche.

Later that evening Jake knocked on the door of the chaplain's room. "Mind a little company?"

"Good grief, no. Come in, Jake, come in." The chaplain beckoned Jake forward. "How on earth they expect me to sleep so much is beyond me."

"I can't stay long," Jake said, drawing up a chair. "Pierre's waiting for me downstairs."

"Nothing could help pass the time better than a chance to be of use to somebody," Chaplain Fox said. "What's on your mind?"

Jake recounted the discussion with Colonel Beecham and the others. "I'm beginning to think there really may be something to all this. And it's got me wondering. I kept thinking about all those kids, and what they've got to look forward to, growing up in a place like this."

But Chaplain Fox did not reply directly. Instead, he watched Jake for a long moment. "Is that the only thing that's bothering you?" he asked.

Jake sighed and examined his hands in his lap. He shook his head.

"Is it Sally?"

A nod this time.

"Do you love her, Jake?"

Another nod.

The chaplain leaned back and said to the ceiling, "Sally is a wonderful girl. She has so much going for her — gorgeous looks, a wonderful smile, brains, a good heart."

"I know," Jake said quietly.

"But she still has not come to terms with her past, Jake. You know that as well as I do. She holds on to her pain, and do you know why?"

"She's still in love with him," Jake replied.

"Of course she is. She will love him until the day she dies. But that doesn't mean that she has to stop living, not unless she chooses to."

"Are you sure you should be telling me this?" Jake asked.

"Sally and I have often spoken this way. I'm quite sure she would agree to my sharing it with you, and if not, then it's my fault, not yours. No, our dear Sally is frightened, Jake. She has loved and lost, and the pain has seared her deeply.

I believe that she sees in you the opportunity to love again, and is terrified."

"Scared of me? I'd never do anything to hurt her."

"Not willingly, no. But you're a strong man, Jake. A man of action. A man of power. She is both attracted to you and desperately afraid that you will take some risk, make some wild and dangerous step that will take you away from her." He watched Jake's reaction. "Do you see what I am saying?"

Jake nodded slowly. "She pushes me away so completely that I think maybe it would be better for both of us if I stopped trying."

"Safer, perhaps, but not better. Not for her, in any case. I have no fear for you, Jake. None at all. You will weather this storm. But Sally may not. Beneath that rough exterior is a sad and lonely young woman. I think she needs you, Jake. More than she realizes."

"I wish it were true."

"I'm fairly certain that it is," Chaplain Fox replied. "I fear that if she succeeds in pushing you away, she will return home and find what she thinks she needs. A safe man, one who never takes any risks whatsoever. Someone who always wears a hat when it's raining, who does everything by the book, who wants nothing more than to live a life of domestic tranquility. Sally is not that sort of girl, no matter how much she might try to convince herself otherwise. You've seen how she is, Jake. You know. She would be smoth-

183

ered by such an existence. Something of the nervous beauty we both admire in her would be extinguished. I fear the fire and depth within Sally would simply fade away."

Jake ran his hands over his face. "I wish I knew what to do."

"Be strong," Chaplain Fox replied. "Do you have a Bible?"

"Somewhere."

"I suggest you take it out and read it. Study the words of other wise men, men of strength who also loved God. Read about men and women who found the ability to withstand adversity by placing their trust in Him. Start with Proverbs, then the first book of Kings, some of the Psalms, the gospel of John, then the letter to the Romans."

"And then report back to you in the morning, right?"

Chaplain Fox smiled. "Ask the Lord to guide you. Not to gain what you want, though. You need to understand from the very outset, Jake, that He is not some bellboy, at your beck and call. Ask Him to *guide* you. Ask Him to show you how you can serve Him and so come to know your full potential, your true destiny. For that glorious completeness can only come to those who have given their lives to Christ."

"That's a big step," he murmured.

"The fact that you see it that way is a good sign," Chaplain Fox replied. "Whether or not this will bring the answer you hope for, I cannot say. That will depend on Sally's own reaction, and whether or not she, too, is willing to look honestly at herself. But whatever happens, Jake, you will know peace. That I can promise you from the depths of my own experience. You will know peace, and you will know the certainty of His glorious presence in your life."

Chapter Sixteen

Jake did not like mornings. Given the choice, he would have preferred to begin his days around noon. A slow gradual rise to consciousness, followed by a cup of good strong coffee taken on the back stoop. Preferably alone. Jake saw no earthly reason to include other people too soon. His motor took a while to warm up.

Which was why, when the soldier standing guard duty pounded on their door, Jake could only manage a moan.

"Captain Burnes. Sorry to bother you, but you've got visitors, sir."

To Jake's befuddled mind, the soldier did not sound sorry at all. In fact, it sounded distinctly as if he had spent much of the night searching for just such an excuse to go out and bother somebody. After all, if he had to stay awake for guard duty, why should anybody else have a decent night's sleep?

Jake groped around, then realized that his gun was in his locker. Too far to lunge.

"Sir, are you there?"

Jake tasted the roof of his mouth and wondered

why it had the distinct flavor of boot leather. He croaked, "Tell 'em to come back in the morning."

"It is morning, sir."

"Wha' time is it?"

"Just gone five, sir."

Jake groaned again.

"Sir, it's some kids. I think you'll want to see them."

Jake found the strength to open one eye. He sought out Pierre's bunk. No help there. Gentle snores emanated from beneath his friend's blanket. "You got any java in the guardhouse?"

"Just the dregs, sir. The pot's been cooking all night. It'll look like tar and taste like, well, I personally wouldn't give it to my dog, sir."

"Sounds about right," Jake said, fumbling for his pants. "Go get me a cup."

The corporal came trotting back just as Jake pushed through the door. "Here you go, sir. Don't say I didn't warn you."

Jake took a slug, and shuddered as the tarry black liquid slid down and lit a fire in his belly. "This had better be good, Corporal."

"Sir, these kids showed up about an hour ago," the corporal replied, scampering alongside Jake. "I recognized a couple of them from the infirmary — I put in some hours helping out there. I was afraid if they stood out there much longer we'd have to put them back in there again. I tried to shoo them off, but they'd just back off a pace and say, 'Kapitän Burnes.' Like that. I don't speak

Kraut, so there wasn't a whole lot else I could find out."

"How many are there?"

"Three up by the gate, some more back by the treeline, I'd guess somewhere around two dozen." The corporal cast him a worried glance. "Hope I did right, waking you up, sir."

"You did fine, Corporal." Jake handed him the empty cup as they rounded the corner and arrived at the main gates.

The camp was enveloped by the utter dark of night's final hour, save for the searchlights reaching from each guard tower. The lights flanking the main gates were trained on a trio of boys wrapped in blankets and oversized greatcoats and stomping their feet to ward off the heavy chill.

"All right, Corporal," Jake said. "Open the gates."

"Sir, Sergeant Morrows explicitly ordered us not to allow either you or Captain Servais to go anywhere outside the camp without an armed escort." When he saw that Jake was about to protest, he pleaded, "Please, sir. If Sarge hears I let you go out there alone he'll have me on spud detail from now 'til kingdom come."

"All right, soldier," Jake relented. "Just stay back a few steps. These boys are very —" He searched for the right word, but could only come up with, "shy."

At the sound of Jake's voice, Karl had become fully alert. When the gates were pulled back and Jake walked through, he said, "Tell them to re-

188

direct those blasted lights."

"But, sir —"

"Play them out beyond us," Jake commanded. "And don't worry. With those kids in the trees nobody is about to sneak up on us."

"Okay, sir," he said doubtfully, and called to the watchtowers.

The proximity of the light made the darkness even more complete. Karl moved farther away from the corporal, and motioned for Jake to follow. When the soldier started along behind him, Jake ordered, "Stay where you are, Corporal."

"But, sir —"

"That's an order, soldier."

"Yessir." Resigned, he stepped back.

The other two boys moved up alongside, effectively blocking Karl and Jake from view. Karl cast a furtive glance around, then announced quietly in German, "I have been busy, Captain."

"Call me Jake," he replied, thinking that anything was better than *Fremder*. "And you shouldn't be out here. You'll just make yourself sick again."

"No more sickness. I become strong. Every day I am better."

Jake inspected the boy's face in the spotlight's reflected glare. "You look better. Not well, but better. You still have to take care of yourself."

"I take care. Just as you say, Captain. I take great care."

"Jake," he corrected.

Karl pointed to the soldiers behind them and demanded, "Those men, they also call you Jake?"

189

"Captain or sir," Jake relented.

"So. I take great care, Captain. And I do as I say."

"You've heard something?"

"I hear much, Captain. Hear much, see much, learn much." Karl's eyes darted once more around the camp and the encircling trees. Then he bent and opened his blanket. A dull glint of yellow flashed from around his neck. "And do more, Captain. Much more. I do what I say. I *find.*"

"Captain Burnes," Colonel Beecham intoned, once Jake had completed his report, "I don't know whether to have you decorated or taken outside and shot."

"Maybe you should do both," Pierre murmured.

"The same holds true for you, Captain Servais."

"I slept through the entire incident, Colonel."

"That's no excuse," the colonel barked. "And as for you, Miss Anders, either you wipe that silly smirk off your face or I'll string you up alongside these two."

"Aye, aye, sir," Sally agreed. "Smirk dead and buried."

Colonel Beecham scowled at the coil of gold rope piled in the center of his desk. "Now what on earth am I to do with this?"

Jake began, "My advice, sir —"

"When I want your advice I'll ask for it, Captain. No, belay that. When I ask for your advice,

190

I order you not to give it."

"Yessir."

The necklace was of woven red and yellow gold thread. Each hollow in its carefully knotted length was filled with a blood-red ruby. The total weight exceeded half a pound.

"Did the boys say whether there was any more where this came from?"

Jake remained silent as ordered.

"Watch yourself, Captain. You are about a hairsbreadth from a firsthand look at the here-after."

"Sir," Jake replied, "I really don't see how we can refuse Karl's offer."

"You don't, eh."

"Nossir."

"All right, then." The colonel picked up the coil and let it cascade through his grasp. "Run it by me one more time."

"Karl says he has found the man who runs the smuggling ring. He and his gang managed to get this from him — don't ask me how. All he would tell me is that the shadows of this city are his friends. Anyway, Karl wants to be paid for the information. Part will go directly to him and his gang, and part to the other gangs that have helped out. The chaplain and I are supposed to dispense the funds."

"How much?" The colonel groaned.

"Ten thousand dollars."

"Good grief! Why not make it ten million? I'd have just about as much chance finding it."

"Yessir, I told him that," Jake replied calmly. "Karl will wait until the goods have been collected by our men — if we give our word that he will receive either the money or half of everything we gain from the arrests. The choice is ours, not his."

Colonel Beecham stared at him from beneath grizzled brows. "That boy is willing to trust us?"

"Not us," Pierre corrected. "He trusts Jake, and only Jake."

"What about this idea of spreading the dough around all the other kids?"

"I wondered about that too, sir," Jake replied. "It appears that during his stint in the hospital, Karl started growing a conscience."

"He's always had one," Sally countered. "He's finally found somebody to use as an example."

"All right," Beecham said. "I've got meetings scheduled with the brass in Frankfurt this afternoon. The plane's due here in two hours. I'll try this out on them and see what they say."

"Quietly, please, sir," Jake asked.

"A big amen to that," Sally agreed. "Make sure they understand this has to be kept quiet. There'd be a real explosion if Connors were to catch wind of this."

"Leave it with me. Connors isn't the only one with allies in the top brass. I'll do my utmost to make sure this thing stays under wraps." He looked at Jake and said, "Burnes, I'm leaving you in charge."

"Me, sir?"

192

"I know, I know, it's against my better judgment too. But O'Reilly is coming with me, and Saunders is still laid up." Major O'Reilly was the colonel's second in command. Captain Saunders, head of administration, was down with inflammation of an old chest wound.

"Sir, I'll try —"

"Spare me," the colonel growled. "Just try and keep the base intact. Do you think that's within your power?"

"Yessir, I'm certain of it, sir."

"We'll see." Beecham looked doubtful. "I keep asking myself how much damage one man can make in one day. But I've learned not to underestimate you, Burnes."

"Thank you, sir. I guess."

Jake took to carrying the little pocket New Testament around with him, pulling it out and glancing through it when he had a free moment. Most of it seemed to be just a jumble of old words, incomprehensible sayings, and strange commands that did not seem to have much to do with any problem he faced. But he drew comfort from the act of reading, not so much at the time, but afterward. There was a different flavor to the hours of that day, despite the fact that he felt like a blind man when the Book was in his hands.

That afternoon Sally found him bent over the text in the infirmary's cramped waiting room. "What have you got there, soldier?"

"Nothing," he said, embarrassed. He jammed

it back into his pocket and buttoned down the flap. "The chaplain's asleep."

"Not anymore. I just went up to see him. I walked right by you, but you were so caught up you didn't notice me."

"That's not possible."

"How easily they forget." She pointed at his pocket. "What is it?"

"Nothing, Sally. Just a Bible."

"Just, the man says. Is this the chaplain's idea?"

"Who else's?"

"You'd better watch it, soldier. You've got all the makings of a great man."

Jake glanced around the room. "Who are you talking to, Sally?"

"I'm talking to you," she said. "Do you know what we are, Jake Burnes?"

"Misguided fools?" he suggested. "Poor lost souls?"

She stepped up close to him and said, "We are friends."

"I'm happy for that," Jake said quietly. "But I can't help wishing for more."

"Don't look down on friendship," she countered. "Most people go through their whole lives without one true friend of the other sex."

Jake thought about that and then said what came naturally to his mind. "Seems to me friendship would be a nice way to start something deeper."

She pulled away from him. "That's the problem with wisdom. Sometimes it comes out with the very last thing you want to hear." She started for the door. "I'm off to sort through some papers. Go see the chaplain, soldier. Tell him I said to watch it with the wisdom. You've got too much of it already."

"That woman certainly needs a friend," Chaplain Fox said, after Jake had told him of their conversation. "Friendship is such a serious responsibility, though, I sometimes wonder whether people would accept the challenge if they really knew what they were letting themselves in for."

Jake inspected the man resting comfortably in the elevated bed. There seemed to be a marked improvement in his condition since the day before. A number of his bruises were more pronounced today, but his entire demeanor had been helped by the night's rest. "I've met some strange ducks in this war, Chaplain. But I do believe you take the cake."

Fox smiled. "I once heard an old pastor describe himself as nothing more than a simple truth-teller. That is the ideal I set for my life. Just to tell people the truth."

"What if they don't want to hear it?"

"Sometimes what people object to isn't so much the truth itself as the way it's communicated," Chaplain Fox replied. "I believe God does not use the From-On-High routine with us very often, because being talked down to makes the message much harder to swallow. No, instead He uses plain, simple folk like you and me. And He tells us to be humble in everything we do and say. So I find a lot of people willing to listen to me. They may disagree, but that is their choice. At least I have done my bit."

"Maybe God uses you as His errand boy," Jake said. "But I doubt if He's gotten all that much out of me."

"Oh, I don't know." The clear gaze rested on him. "Take care of your new friend, will you, Jake?"

"I'll try," he said without conviction. "I don't know whether she'll let me."

"Just live up to your own responsibilities, and learn to give the rest to God's care." The chaplain turned his face toward the ceiling. "If you'll excuse me, I think perhaps I'll rest a little now. All this truth-telling is exhausting."

Sally found Jake later that afternoon checking preparations at the feeding station. "Beecham's come through again, soldier."

"He's back already?"

"Next thing to it," she replied, waving a yellow paper. "Take a look at this."

Jake wiped greasy hands on his apron, accepted the cable, and read, "Held over here. Tell Burnes he has green light. Proceed with caution. Wolves about. Beecham."

"That's it, then," Jake said, feeling the familiar old pre-combat adrenaline rush.

Sally was watching him. "I assume you read the closing lines."

"I'll take care, Sally. I promise."

Her gaze turned flat, opaque. "Yeah. Right," she said. "Tell me another one, soldier. You can hardly wait for the chance to go marching into battle."

"I am going to take care," Jake repeated, putting as much feeling into it as he could. "For you as much as for me."

The hardness melted away, exposing the wounds of another time. "Oh, Jake," she sighed. "Why do you have to say those things."

"You know why," he replied. "Now go tell Pierre to join me. He's playing Papa in the crèche."

Sally searched his face and started to say something, then stopped, wheeled around, and scrambled across the rubble heap. Jake watched with a hungry heart as she left.

"That's some dame, sir," Sergeant Morrows said, stirring a steaming cauldron nearby. He was grinning from ear to ear as he voiced the words.

"Hand that ladle to somebody else and come over here, Sergeant."

"Aw, hey, I didn't mean anything by that, sir. Can't you take a joke?"

Jake turned on his heel and stomped out of range. Sergeant Morrows followed reluctantly. He stopped a pace away and protested, "Honest, sir —"

"As far as anybody else is concerned I am chewing you out," Jake said softly. "So keep your face screwed up."

Morrows ducked his head, kicked at a stone, said, "Yessir."

"I believe I can trust you, Sergeant."

"I'd like to think so, sir."

"Can you find another dozen or so men who know how to button up their lips and keep them that way?"

"As many as you like, sir."

"We're going on a raiding party, Sergeant. As soon as it's dark." Jake glanced at his watch. "That gives you less than two hours to round them up and get them ready."

Morrows looked as if he had just sucked the juice from an overripe lemon, but nothing could hide the gleam in his eye. "Is it to do with the treasure, sir?"

"Could be, Sergeant." Jake scratched his face to maintain the scowl. "This has got to be on the QT, Sergeant. Strictly confidential. The colonel knows about it. He's given go-ahead. The danger doesn't come from him."

"I understand perfectly, sir." Morrows was having trouble restraining himself. "Where's the rendezvous point?"

"At the lay-by between HQ and the main camp. In ninety minutes."

"We'll be there, sir. Armed and ready for the dance."

"Go to it, then." Jake spotted Pierre and waved him over. "Servais and I have got to see our contact."

Sergeant Morrows snapped to attention and bellowed out, "Sir, yessir! It won't happen again, sir!"

"Ninety minutes, Sergeant," Jake said quietly. "Be on time."

Chapter Seventeen

Karl pointed through the blackness to a single glowing window. "He is in there."

They were gathered on a city street reduced to heaps of rubble by the allied bombardment. They huddled in what had once been someone's basement, now a hole partially filled with the remains of the house that had stood overhead. The building across the street had fared better. The walls appeared to be intact, and the window they watched held signs of great wealth in war-ravaged Germany — glass panes and curtains.

Jake turned to Sergeant Morrows and said in a muted voice, "Have your men fan out. You take the rear detail, circle around, and make sure every possible avenue of escape is covered."

Morrows squinted into the darkness, measuring the ground with an experienced eye, and said, "Fifteen minutes max."

"The signal to move will be a whistle. Remember, we want this man alive. Nobody is to shoot unless the other side shoots first."

"I've spelled it out personal to the men, sir."

Jake spent another moment going over everything in his mind once more. Then he said, "All right. Get going."

Sergeant Morrows rose from his crouch, gave the signal. They started forward in utter stealth. But the rubble beneath their feet was loose; as one soldier scrambled out, a rock went ricocheting down to the bottom, where it hit against a piece of roofing, then splashed into a puddle with a noise that seemed to shatter the night.

Each man froze where he was. All eyes remained on the window.

A second crack of light appeared as the door of the dwelling opened. A figure came into view, silhouetted by the interior lighting. He stood and looked straight at them. Jake resisted the urge to duck, to move, to hide.

Then the impossible happened.

A rasping man's voice spoke at a level barely above a whisper, yet loud enough to be heard clearly in the freezing quiet. "*Bitte kommen Sie vorwärts, Herr Kapitän Burnes.* I have been expecting you."

"I knew it was you because the other hunters would not have stopped at only one item," the man continued on in German, his voice strangely hoarse.

"I was told you had so much treasure stuffed in your chests that you'd never notice if one piece was gone," Jake countered. He sat alone in a cluttered parlor. His men surrounded the building. Everywhere Jake looked there were signs of wealth, relative to the rest of the German nation that winter evening — four solid walls, a dry chamber, the remains of a meal on a simple wooden table, a fire in the grate.

"Ah, there the mistake was made," came the whispered reply. "My training stressed thoroughness in all things, Herr Kapitän."

The man limped to one corner and hefted a high-caliber rifle equipped with a sniper's scope. "You should understand that."

"You shot at me in the forest," Jake said.

"Wrong, Captain. I shot at a tree. If I had shot at you we would not be speaking together now."

The right side of the man's lower face and much of his neck had been scooped out, as though someone had attacked it with a giant razor-sharp spoon. He swallowed with difficulty, and spoke only with great effort. Jake pointed at the wound and asked, "Where did you pick that up?"

"On the eastern front," he exhaled. "I was proving to be quite a bother, so the Russians moved up their artillery and opened fire."

"You're lucky to be here."

"In more ways than one, Captain. When the rout began, and the Nazi army was forced to retreat across frozen tundra with nothing to eat for days on end, I was safely back in my beloved Badenburg, settled in a comfortable hospital bed."

"So how did you get into the treasure-smuggling game?"

"There were almost no able-bodied men available toward the end of the war," he replied. "Even the severely wounded like me were forced into service. Not in uniform, however. No. I became servant to one of the ranking SS officers."

"I'm beginning to get the picture."

"There were many Nazi leaders who had holiday residences here, or hunting lodges just outside of town. It was expected of them, you see. This was the gathering point for the Nazi elite."

"And you came to know them all."

"Many of them, yes. A servant is able to see much, especially when he has so clearly given his all to the Fatherland." Slack facial muscles pulled together in a parody of a smile. "And when he can be trusted to remain silent."

"So you knew where they hid their treasure," Jake said.

"Not so fast, Captain. Not so fast. There is more to this than you realize."

"But there is treasure."

Again the rictal smile. "Indeed there is."

"Where?"

"Just over our heads. Some of it, anyway."

Jake resisted an urge to search the ceiling. "Why didn't you just cut and run?"

"Your patrols have become too thorough, Captain. My three best men are now sitting in various jails, charged with smuggling."

"They were caught on the way back in from dropping off their treasures in France," Jake guessed, and pointed with his chin to the half-finished meal. "Probably carrying contraband to make your lives here easier."

"Thank heaven for such minor miracles, yes?" He walked toward the wall cabinet, his left foot scraping across the floor. "A glass of schnapps?"

"I don't think we're going to be around long enough for that, thanks." Jake inspected the man. "So you knew I was coming and didn't run. You've got to admit, that sounds a little strange."

"Not if you knew what I know, Captain."

"Which is?"

"I shall come to that in a moment." He filled two glasses and handed one over. "Please."

Jake accepted the drink and set it down beside him. "Your moment's up."

"The American way, straight to the point, yes?" The man stomped over and sat facing Jake. "Very well, Captain. What I have upstairs is only the tip of the iceberg."

"What are you saying?"

"Personal effects some of the officers were in too much of a hurry to take with them." He gave another death's-head grin. "Or maybe their destination did not permit it."

"So you searched through their things and rounded up this little trove?"

"A few paintings which survived the bombardment, some decorative items they simply had to have on display, jewels intended for some fair neck or hand or ear." The man leaned forward. "But there is yet another stash, Captain. One which I have been unable to tap. Their savings, so to speak. Not what found its way to the government's own hoards. No. What I speak of are the precious items they chose to keep for themselves."

"And you know where all these things are buried."

"I do."

"And you want something in exchange."

"Naturally."

Jake thought it over. "What is your name?"

"Konrad," he replied, giving a small, seated bow. "Jurgen Konrad, at your service."

"So what's the deal, Herr Konrad?"

"There is so much treasure hidden away, Captain. So much you cannot even begin to imagine."

"So?"

"I am tired of running, Captain," Konrad replied. "I lost my youth in the war. I only want the conqueror's permission to live in peace. To have papers. And enough money to enjoy this freedom. I will give you the hidden treasure, Captain, if you will allow me to keep the small trinkets I have upstairs for myself."

"Some loose change for your remaining years."

"Compared to what remains concealed," Konrad replied, "these are mere trifles."

"You know I can't agree to anything like that without authorization."

"Of course. You will naturally have to take me into custody until an agreement can be reached."

"And the treasure upstairs," Jake added. "Do you really trust me that much?"

"The entire town speaks of Captain Jake Burnes. I know you through what I have heard."

"You don't know a thing about me," Jake contradicted.

"I know you are a man of honor," Konrad replied. "Under the circumstances, it is all that matters."

Chapter Eighteen

Jake called Pierre and Sally into Colonel Beecham's office that evening. Sitting there surrounded by the colonel's things gave them a reassuring sense of being under his direction. Since receiving the cable, they had heard nothing. Sally's urgent entreaties over the telephone had yielded no response. Colonel Beecham was not available. Period.

"At least our German's safe," Jake offered. They had stashed the man upstairs in one attic cubbyhole, the treasure in another. A pair of soldiers stood guard in the hall outside, another on the next floor's landing, still more in pairs outside. "Never had so many soldiers volunteer for guard duty."

"Do you really think Connors and his men were that near to closing in?" Sally asked.

Jake shrugged. "Herr Konrad thought so, and right now, that's what matters."

"What do you mean?"

"I want him to feel that we are honoring his trust in us," Jake explained.

"Honest Jake the treasure dealer. You take the cake, soldier."

"He's put his life and fortune in our hands," Jake protested. "We owe him that much."

"It was a good idea to post the lookout by his residence," Servais told them. "We'll know soon enough if Konrad had reason to fear the MPs."

"Make sure those boys are relieved every couple of hours," Jake told him. "It's too cold a night for them to stand still any longer than that."

"Aye, aye, sir."

Jake looked chagrined. "Did I sound too much like the colonel?"

Pierre shrugged. "Somebody has to be in charge until Beecham returns. If that German soldier upstairs will trust you with his life, why shouldn't I?"

"Thanks, Pierre," Jake said quietly.

"I wonder how much that treasure upstairs is worth," Sally mused.

"Hard to say," Pierre answered. "The war has depressed prices tremendously. But I would still say enough for a man to live a very long and comfortable life."

In the old man's attic there had been six paintings, two of them fire-blackened but still recognizable as the work of masters. Three massive Persian silk carpets, far too bulky to smuggle out. A pair of silver and crystal candelabras. And four locker-size chests full to the brim with jewelry.

"I thought Morrows was going to burst a gut when he pried off that first lid," Jake recalled.

"I didn't know anybody's eyes could get that

big," Sally agreed, rising to her feet with a yawn. "Well, I'm either going back to bed or sacking out on the floor right here."

"I'll walk you back," Jake offered, and when she did not object, followed her from the room.

They walked the short distance in silence. At the doorway to her billet, she turned and offered a sleepy smile. "Why don't you come up and see me sometime, soldier."

"I wish you meant that," Jake replied in a subdued voice.

The smile and the fatigue slipped away. "Give it time, Jake. Maybe it will happen."

"I hope so."

"I know you do." Softly now. "Dear Jake. Look at how tall you've grown."

"I'm the same height I always was."

"So tall," she repeated. "You positively tower over the other men around here."

"And still I'm not good enough for you," he said with a trace of bitterness.

"Don't say that," she said, but without anger. "Don't ever say that."

"I'll never be able to fill a dead man's shoes, will I?"

"That's not the point, Jake." She gave him a wounded look. "Can you tell me why life has to be so hard?"

"I wish I knew," Jake said, aching for her. Despite the fear and pleading in her eyes, he started toward her. But he drew back when he heard the sound of running feet thundering down the back hallway of the HQ.

Jake turned around. An instant later Pierre slammed back the door. "Red alert, Jake. Let's move out!"

"They hit Konrad's house about three quarters of an hour ago," Pierre said, hustling Jake back into the colonel's office. "When they found the place empty, they went totally berserk."

"Connors' men?" Jake nodded to Morrows, who was standing back waiting anxiously in the outer office. "Come on in, Sergeant."

"Thank you, sir."

"Who else?" Pierre motioned to the two men waiting inside. Both snapped to attention at Jake's entry. "Simpkins and Vance, the soldiers on duty when it happened."

"At ease, men." Reluctantly Jake moved behind the colonel's desk and sat down, making room for the rest. "Colonel Beecham is in Frankfurt," he explained. "He left me in charge during his absence." To his surprise, no one batted an eye at the news.

"Tell him," Servais ordered.

"Sir, we were heads down in the ditch like you ordered. All of a sudden these two trucks and maybe four jeeps —"

"Just the ones we could see," Vance interrupted. "But we could hear shouts and stuff from the road in back. Especially after."

"Right. So out they pile —"

"All MPs?" Jake demanded.

210

"Yessir. That is, all of them had on the white helmets and bands."

"Go on."

"So out they come on the bounce, like I said. And they hit the house six ways from Sunday, breaking down the door, shining lights everywhere, shattering windows, and poking their rifles in —"

"Just like this gangster film I saw back in the States," Vance offered.

Simpkins turned his way. "Who's telling this story, you or me?"

"You're doing fine, soldier," Jake said. "Carry on."

"Right, sir. So then there's this shout from inside, 'He's not here.' And somebody from outside called back, 'And the loot?' And the guy inside shouted, 'Gone!' Then, sir, this guy outside, he just goes bananas. Stomping around, cursing, screaming to wake the dead —"

"Woulda made a drill sergeant blush," Vance added. "Mentioned your name a few times. I'd just as soon not tell you what he said."

"That's all right, Simpkins," Jake said mildly. "I can imagine."

"Yessir. So then he sends the ones who speak Kraut to question everybody in all the surrounding buildings, to see if maybe anybody saw anything. And the other guys started combing the area. We couldn't get out any sooner, sir. They were all around us."

"We can thank our lucky stars there ain't no

streetlights, sir," Vance agreed. "Two of them guys almost stepped on my toes, they was so close."

"Yeah, sir, we just hunkered down in the pit there and waited them out."

"And listened."

"Sir, you can't imagine the noise. I mean, people wailing and moaning and carrying on up and down the street, all these MPs shouting and cursing. I doubt most of the Krauts had any idea what was going on."

"They didn't have to," Jake said grimly. "Being awakened in the middle of the night like that probably reminded them of their worst nightmare."

"Yessir, I guess so. Anyway, these guys stick around a while, then all start coming back to that one who's still kicking up a storm around the jeep. We didn't wait to see what happened next. Soon as they were back on the other side of the street, we hightailed it outta there."

"Good work, you two. Better get yourselves some shut-eye."

"Yessir. Thank you, sir."

"Morrows, think maybe you could get Cookie out of bed?"

"No problem, sir."

"Ask him to make a couple of big pots of coffee, maybe some soup would be better, and a big box of sandwiches. Have your men take them over to the neighborhood the MPs just terrorized. Does anybody in your squad speak German?"

"Don't think so, sir."

Jake took out a piece of paper, scribbled furiously and handed it over. "Have them show this around the street. My guess is, half the neighborhood will still be up talking about it, now that the danger's over. Tell them to show the paper to everybody. It basically just apologizes for the disturbance."

"A good idea, Jake," Pierre murmured.

"Yessir, sure is," Morrows agreed, inspecting the paper. "A little PR at a time like this couldn't hurt anybody."

"I just want them to understand that we are sorry the MPs got out of line." Jake looked at Sally standing in the doorway. "Would you mind putting off your sleep for just a little while longer, and see if you can find Beecham for us?"

She spun on her heel and was gone without a word.

Jake looked at Pierre. "You'd better tell the guard detail to be on full alert."

Pierre was on his feet. "I'll send another squad up to the base as well."

"Good thinking," Jake agreed, and rose. "I guess it's time I had a little talk with our friend upstairs."

The German listened in watchful silence as Jake related the developments. "You see," he rasped, when Jake was finished, "I was right after all."

"They won't stop now," Jake said.

"You know my conditions," the man replied in his throaty whisper. "The only reason I spoke to you at all was to obtain my request."

"How much have you already shipped across the border," Jake demanded.

The man hesitated, then replied, "About as much as what you have here. Perhaps a little more. But not much. And there were three other partners to take care of."

"This isn't all the treasure you've collected, is it?"

Konrad became very still, his eyes blank.

"You didn't collect everything in one place," Jake persisted. "And I imagine there are several bombed-out mansions you haven't gotten around to looting yet. You probably hit the ones that were the least damaged, with the largest caches of valuables and in the most accessible places. It must be hard-going, trying to sift through all that rubble in the dark. Especially now that all but one of your partners are sitting in a jail somewhere."

The man remained mute.

"I thought so," Jake said. "You're trapped, aren't you?"

"Almost as trapped as you, Captain," Jurgen Konrad replied.

"I know where you could pick up some more partners fast," Jake continued. "Partners who can run fast, dig for hours on end, even crawl in and out of upstairs windows without being caught."

The gaze flickered. "You cannot be serious."

"Partners you can trust," Jake continued. "If they gave you their word, you could trust them with your very life. I would."

"Then you are a very simple man, Captain."

Jake shook his head. "I have worked with them. I have come to know them well."

"As well as any human being can know an animal."

"They are not animals," Jake said sharply. "They are survivors. Their way of life has been shaped by events beyond their control. They have faced difficulties that should have killed them, and yet they survived."

The German searched Jake's face and gave his head a slight shake. "This is so strange."

"What is?"

"You really do care for these cellar children, don't you, Captain?"

"They are worthy of your trust. And they will help you."

"Very well, Captain," came the rasped reply. "I will think over your words."

Jake nodded. "As to this other matter —"

"It exists," Konrad insisted. "The treasure is there."

"It's unlikely to be there for long," Jake pointed out.

"I understand your concern," Konrad replied. "But my demands must be met."

"Perhaps others know of this treasure," Jake pressed.

"Few ever knew of it," Konrad whispered. "And even fewer still came through alive."

"If one did, there may be others," Jake went on. "Any moment now, the MPs may stumble upon someone ready to tell the tale."

"Why are you speaking to me like this, Captain?" Konrad demanded. "You do not strike me as one who is greedy for treasure."

"I want nothing for myself," Jake asserted.

"Then why do you not simply agree to my demands and let us get on with it?"

"Because I do not have the authority," Jake confessed. "And my superior officer is not here."

"Contact him, then."

"I have tried. I am trying. I cannot find him."

"And this concerns you."

"Very much," Jake said grimly.

"You think others may be responsible for his disappearance?"

"I don't know what to think."

Konrad sipped from his water jug, making loud swallowing sounds that were painful in Jake's ears. He set down the jug and breathed heavily, as though the effort of drinking had exhausted him. Then he said, "What is it you want?"

"I have promised to reward my young German helpers," Jake said. "I need to take their payment from your hoard, to ensure that whatever happens they are properly compensated."

"A man of his word," the German said. "I was right to trust you, Captain."

"The soldiers who are working on this project

also have a right to expect something," Jake continued.

"How much do you want?"

Jake thought it over and decided, "Everything we have taken from your attic and secured here."

"Impossible."

"You keep everything else."

"And if I am unable to travel to France to collect the proceeds from what has already been sold? Or retrieve anything more for myself here? You see the condition the war has left me in. I would be signing my own death warrant." Konrad shook his head. "The carpets, perhaps."

"Not enough," Jake replied. "A full chest. That is the least I need."

Konrad thought for a moment, then asked, "What about my papers?"

Jake thought it over, and decided that if he was going out on a limb so far, he might as well start sawing away. "I will go down and have them issued immediately."

"Also," Konrad went on, "you must have my partners released from your jails. Give me pen and paper so that I may write down their names."

"I can ask," Jake replied, fishing in his shirt pocket. "And I will. But I cannot order it. The officer in charge may be willing to do it as a special favor. But I can't promise anything."

Konrad considered this. "You will do this immediately?"

"I will write the letters tonight," Jake replied. "And send the couriers off at first light."

The German inspected him carefully. "You are taking a risk, yes?"

"This entire episode will probably cost me my rank," Jake replied soberly. "Maybe earn me a tour of duty behind bars."

"Then why do you do this?"

"I have my reasons," Jake said, rising to his feet. "When can I have your answer?"

"In the morning," Konrad replied. "I shall think about your request and tell you my decision in the morning. Perhaps your colonel will have come back by then."

"Perhaps," Jake said, unconvinced.

"You think he has run away and left you with all the risks?"

"No," Jake replied, definite for the first time that night. "Colonel Beecham is a good man."

"He may be, Captain," Konrad said, stretching out on his mattress. "But my trust lies in you. Good-night."

Jake marched back downstairs, stopped by Sally's door, and asked, "Any word?"

"He seems to have vanished from the face of the earth," Sally replied. She ran tired hands through her hair. "It's as if he had never even existed."

"Go get some sleep," he told her.

"What about you?" she responded. "You look ready to join the ranks of the walking wounded."

"That was an order," he said.

"Well, in that case —" She groaned her way to her feet, patting his arm as she passed on the way to the door. "Good-night, Commander."

"I'm just a simple soldier," Jake corrected.

"Not anymore," she replied. "Try to get some rest, Jake. From the looks of things, tomorrow is going to be a long day."

But when at last he was bedded down in the HQ's visiting officers' quarters, Jake found himself unable to calm his mind. As he rolled restlessly back and forth, he heard Pierre's voice calling softly through the darkness, "Are you asleep?"

"No."

"Worried about the treasure?"

Jake shook his head, then realized that Pierre could not see him. "No."

"What, then?"

"Sally," he confessed.

"I suppose I should be jealous," Pierre said. "I confess that I am not."

"Girl back home?"

"There was, back when the war began. But I lost her."

"Sorry to hear that," Jake said, and recalled his own loss.

"When I think of her, which I try to do as seldom as possible, it is with great regret."

"I know what you mean."

"Yes, I believe you. Perhaps that is why I can speak with you, that and the cloak of darkness which surrounds us. It hides my shame from the world."

"Shame over what?"

"It is said that some people are destined to love only once. I fear that I am not only such a man, but, I also loved the wrong woman. A lovely lady, truly beautiful. Half French, half Moroccan. But also treacherous. It still pains me deeply to think of her. Perhaps it always will."

"I know it's hard to believe," Jake said, and laced his fingers behind his head. "But you'll get over it. I did."

Pierre was silent for a moment, then said, "I marvel at you sometimes, my friend."

"Me? Why?"

"Because you *care*." Pierre's bed creaked as he shifted around. "You have seen the worst of war and still you are alive inside. How have you managed this?"

"I don't know that I have," Jake replied quietly.

"You have, my friend. I see it in your eyes. I see it in the way you look at Sally. I see it when you are with the children. I have no doubts. None."

"Sometimes," Jake said slowly, "I remember . . . things."

"Ah, yes. Things. I have memories like these as well." The springs squeaked beneath Pierre as he raised himself up on one elbow. The white of his T-shirt and the dog tags hanging around his neck glinted in the faint light coming through their window. "I was seventeen when the Nazis invaded my country and made a laughingstock of the French army. I have never felt such helplessness as I did in those days, glued to the wireless, unable to do anything but cry and curse as Petain announced his capitulation to the Boche."

"Where were you raised?" Jake asked.

"Montpellier. West of Marseille. I ran away from home four days later. I caught a freighter to Algiers with a hundred other boys, all of us fired by the rumor that De Gaulle was gathering an expeditionary force to return and liberate my country."

"Did you have any brothers and sisters?"

"One brother. We were twins. He remained behind and joined the Underground. He was caught and shot in the last year of the war." Pierre's voice turned bitter. "I languished in Algiers for two years. Two *years*. I watched my friends give in to the hopelessness and the drink and the emptiness of life. But I fought it, my friend. I fought the only way I knew how. By hating. I hated the life. I hated the heat. I hated the foul things these losers did to their minds and bodies. I hated the politicians and the generals for their endless bickering. And I hated the Boche most of all."

"But you survived," Jake reminded him. "Don't forget that."

"Yes, it's true. But sometimes, Jake, when I look at you and see how you still care, I wonder if perhaps some part of me was destroyed by all that hating. My hatred is gone now. I lost it somewhere on the battlefield. It was burned up in the smoking ruins of another village whose

221

name I don't recall. But nothing has come to take its place, Jake. Inside me now there is only emptiness."

Jake thought of his own struggles. "The chaplain told me to find the answers in prayer."

"Yes?" Pierre swung himself into a seated position. "And what do you think of that?"

"I don't know," Jake confessed. "But maybe I'll give it a try."

"But why, Jake? If you are not sure, how can you risk so much on the ramblings of a priest?"

"Because," Jake said, choosing his words carefully, "every time I look inside myself or let myself care, what I feel most is pain."

"Yes," Pierre murmured. "This pain I know very well. Too well."

Jake turned toward his unseen friend, an appeal in his voice. "I've got to try to find some way to be healed, Pierre. I've got to make this pain go away before I can start over."

"And you truly think this pain can be healed?" Pierre demanded.

"I've got to try," Jake repeated quietly.

Pierre slid back down, sighed, and said to the dark night, "Then perhaps I shall give this a try as well."

Chapter Nineteen

"You have heard from your colonel?" Konrad demanded when Jake arrived the next morning.

"Not a word," Jake replied, making no attempt to conceal his anxiety. He handed Konrad a steaming mug of coffee and sat down across the table from him. "The couriers have left for the border internment stations. I can't promise anything, but at least we are trying to have your partners released."

The German sipped, making his painful swallowing effort, then rasped, "But I have agreed to nothing."

Jake reached into his pocket and handed over a sheaf of folded papers. "Call it a sign of good will," he said. "Your documents, as promised."

With slow, deliberate motions, Konrad set down his cup and opened the papers. He looked at them for a long moment, then, without raising his head, said, "Very well, Captain. I agree."

Jake leaned back, releasing a sigh. "That's it, then."

The German pulled damaged facial muscles into the semblance of a smile. "No, Captain, that is where you are wrong. It is only the beginning."

When he left Jurgen Konrad's chambers, Jake walked outside for a breath of air. Konrad's news had shaken him to the core. He stepped through the doors into brilliant winter sunlight. It took him a moment to focus. When he did, he found himself staring out over a field of green uniforms. All eyes were upon him.

Sergeant Morrows mounted the stairs. "I guess word got out, sir."

Jake surveyed the throng. "Is anybody shirking their duty?"

"Not so far as I can tell," Pierre replied from below. "I've checked with as many of the department chiefs as I can find."

Jake raised his voice and said, "If anybody is out here expecting to go home rich, you might as well return to your barracks."

No one moved.

"You know how the army works," Jake continued in his parade-ground voice. "Maybe your great-grandchildren might get a penny on the dollar, but it's highly unlikely. If the treasure really is there — and we don't have any guarantee that it exists at all — the bigwigs will be quarreling over it from now 'til doomsday."

The soldiers remained where they were. A voice from somewhere in the crowd called back, "We know that, sir."

"You will all be searched thoroughly," Jake persisted. "Don't think for a minute you'll be able to sneak something out."

They remained a solid wall of fatigue green. "All right," Jake relented. "Captain Servais and Sergeant Morrows will act as liaison. Everybody is dismissed. Platoon leaders, report to the squad room in fifteen minutes. Anybody caught shirking duty will be flailed alive — by me personally. Dismissed."

Jake walked back inside the headquarters building and said to no one in particular, "Would somebody mind telling me what's going on?"

"It's very simple," Sally replied, coming up beside him. "They know a leader when they see one."

Jake unfolded the city map on the colonel's desk. "This is the best we've got?"

Sally nodded. "About a quarter of the streets don't exist anymore. Nothing's there but fields of scrap and waste. Survey has marked most of them."

"All right, then it will just have to do."

"Why couldn't it have been somewhere else?" Pierre muttered to himself.

"Because it isn't," Jake said, his finger tracing possible routes.

"And you're sure this isn't just a ruse?"

"Konrad insists he's giving us the scoop," Jake replied. "He says he even took a shipment in there himself just before the Allies arrived. One of the officers back on leave used him as a pair of trusted hands."

"What was it like?"

"Stolen Nazi loot from floor to ceiling, by the sound of it." Jake covered his own excitement with a scowl. "But you're right. They really picked the spot."

Morrows knocked on the open door. "The men are all assembled, sir."

"Right. Grab that map, Pierre. Anybody seen my hat?"

Sally walked over and handed it to him. "Here you are, sir."

"Thanks. Are you coming?"

"I wouldn't miss it for the world," Sally replied, her eyes bright, "sir."

Jake marched into the meeting hall and straight to the podium. The gathered squad and platoon leaders snapped to attention as he entered. "At ease," he said, taking strength from the fact that his voice remained steady.

He waited until Pierre, Sally, and Morrows were seated. Then he went on. "I've got good news and bad news. The good news is that it appears there is indeed a larger stash of treasure inside the city."

There was a moment's electric silence, then a raised hand. "Yes?"

"How large is large, sir?"

"I don't have the exact figures," Jake replied. "But from the sound of it, big enough to set off alarms from here to Madagascar."

A stir rippled through the group. "Settle down," Jake said. "You haven't heard the bad news yet. And believe me, it couldn't be worse. Captain Servais?"

With Sergeant Morrows' help, Pierre unfolded the large-scale map and held it up against the back wall. Jake walked over and pointed to an area, "The treasure is supposed to be located right here. Does anybody recognize the place?"

People half-rose from their seats as they strained and searched and finally started in alarm. "Sir, isn't that — ?"

"That's right, gentlemen," Jake affirmed. "The treasure is right smack-dab underneath the stockade."

Chapter Twenty

"Nobody moves without an order from me, Sergeant Morrows," Jake said, climbing into the second jeep beside Pierre.

"But, sir —"

"I'll be back," Jake assured him.

"I will personally see to that," Pierre confirmed.

"But just six men, Captain, ain't that —"

"We can't tip them off, Sergeant." Jake stopped further conversation by rapping his knuckles on the side of the jeep. "Let's go."

When they arrived at the feeding station they found it in full swing, manned by the ten men Morrows considered most likely to keep a lid on their excitement. Still, despite the warnings, their arrival caused a major stir.

"Back to your positions, gentlemen," Jake ordered, his voice low. "We are being watched."

On the other side of the street a squad of MPs loitered around a couple of jeeps. They watched Jake's arrival through narrowed eyes, but made no move. Jake helped Sally down from the jeep and murmured, "Do you see Karl?"

"Not yet."

"I'll check around," Pierre said.

"Not alone," Jake reminded him, and turned with Sally toward the crèche.

Inside, all was normal and calm, or as calm as any room could be that held twenty-eight infants under the age of four. Sally was immediately engulfed in a press of little figures, their voices raised, their hands lifted to touch and be recognized and receive attention. Jake stood back and watched the transformation in her face, saw the love shining in her eyes, and felt himself a thousand miles from where he would like to be. When Pierre returned he walked over and asked, "Did you find Karl?"

"Outside. How do you want to handle this?"

"Not here." Jake pulled out pen and paper, scribbled a note, and handed it to Pierre. "Give him that."

When Pierre was gone, Jake turned back to the gathering of happy little girls. "Sally?"

"I think I'll stay awhile, Jake," she replied.

"I'll tell the kitchen detail to pick you up on their way out."

"All right." For a moment, a brief moment that seemed an eternity yet was over as soon as it began, she granted him the same look of love and tenderness she had bestowed upon the little girls. "Take care, Jake."

"I will," he replied, and because he could not say the other things tumbling through his mind, and did not want to risk seeing that look vanish from her eyes, he turned and left.

Jake walked across the vacant lot and pretended to inspect the kitchen. He accepted the smart salutes and brisk replies with an assumed calm. From the corner of his eyes he noted the MPs tracking his every step. When he deemed that the charade had continued long enough, he returned with his guard detail to the jeep.

"Where to?" Pierre asked.

"Head back toward HQ," Jake replied, determinedly keeping his gaze off the MPs. "Take it slow."

They were perhaps three blocks away from the center and rounding a corner when Karl and two of his companions popped up from behind the waist-high remains of a house. "Slower," Jake ordered, and then barked in German, "Move!"

The jeep continued rolling as the trio scrambled over the wall, covered the distance, and piled into the back. Jake signaled to the jeep behind them that all was well, checked swiftly for spying eyes, found none, and shouted, "Go!"

The kids sat bright-eyed and excited as they sped back out of town. Jake directed Pierre to turn down a dirt track not far from the HQ. When the second jeep had halted behind them, Jake turned to Karl and said in German, "We got the man."

"And the treasure, I hope," Karl said in his accustomed sharp tone. But the gleam in his eyes was strong. "The man is nothing without his hoard."

"That too," Jake agreed. "Or part of it, at least."

"And where is the rest?"

"That is what I want to speak to you about," Jake replied, reaching for the map. He folded it out to the appropriate section, pointed to the building with the circle drawn around it, and asked, "Do you know where this is?"

Clearly the boy had never been challenged in this way before. "I don't —"

"The stockade," Jake said.

"Where the white hats gather. Of course." Karl bent over the incomprehensible map. "They have taken the treasure there?"

"Not exactly," Jake replied. "The place used to be a bank. According to Herr Konrad, the bank's vault was in the cellar. What was not so well known was that they had also constructed a second cellar. Directly *underneath* the main vault."

Karl reacted with a hunter's eager tension. "A secret vault."

"Very secret," Jake agreed. "So secret not even the bank employees themselves knew of it."

"How was it reached?"

"Through a tunnel," Jake answered. "This much we know for sure. A tunnel at least forty paces long. With stairs leading to it."

"The man has seen this tunnel?"

"His name is Jurgen Konrad," Jake said. "And the answer is no, not exactly. Toward the end of the war, he was taken down there by his em-

231

ployer, who wished to get an inventory of some of his treasure and to make sure nothing had been stolen. He trusted Konrad enough to enlist his help, but before they began the journey, a hood was placed over Konrad's head. Though he couldn't see he could still hear, and he knows he was led through a narrow concrete tunnel before entering the vault itself."

"So how does he know that the vault is located there?"

"He says he heard them boasting," Jake replied. "Every time the officers would gather and drink too much, their talk would turn at one point or another to the cache beneath the bank."

The girl with Karl demanded, "And the treasure is still there?"

"Konrad's partners kept careful watch as long as they were free," Jake replied. "They hoped that someone would appear and lead them to the tunnel entrance. But not one of the senior officers returned from the last battles. Not one. Konrad believes they have all died or been arrested."

"So you want us to find this tunnel," Karl said.

"I want you to be extremely careful," Jake replied. "You will be walking through enemy territory."

"All life has its dangers, Captain. You should know that." Karl slipped from the jeep. "Do you have our money?"

Jake shook his head. "But I have some of Konrad's treasure in safekeeping for you. Do you want it now?"

"Later, yes. Not now, but later." The young man grinned for the first time Jake could remember. "We make a good team, yes, Captain?"

"A great team," Jake said, and meant it.

"There will be more rewards from this work?"

"Whether or not you succeed," Jake replied, "I will see that you are rewarded."

"We know where to find you," Karl said. He and his gang turned and raced off through the trees.

Chapter Twenty-one

Dusk was gathering when a muffled shout at the HQ's main gate brought Jake running.

Jake found Karl and three friends squatting in the guardhouse, far enough down to be invisible from the outside. Jake stood in the entrance and said to the nearby soldier, "Back up a pace, Corporal, so everybody can see you, and stand at attention. I want any unfriendly eyes to think I'm tearing off a piece of your hide."

"Yessir." The corporal gave a fair imitation of a soldier retreating before a storm of abuse.

"Did anybody else see them?"

"I didn't see them myself, sir. One minute I was looking down a lonesome road, and the next these four come piling in around me. Don't ask me how they got so close, 'cause I sure don't know."

Jake switched into German and said, "The soldier is impressed with your stealth."

"The shadows of this town are my friends," Karl replied. "You are being watched."

"Where?" Jake asked.

"Around the first corner going toward town

234

there is a trail leading off into the woods."

"I know of it."

"They sit in their jeep and talk so anyone can hear," Karl said. "They do not sound happy. They care little for their work."

Jake said to the corporal, "We've got a surveillance team set up around the first bend."

"Doesn't surprise me in the least, sir."

"When we're finished here, go find Captain Servais. Tell him that one of our night patrols ought to take the first dirt track leading off the road into town. Anybody they find should be arrested on sight."

"Yessir. Consider it done."

To Karl he said, "You have found us an entry?"

"I have found many dark holes," Karl said wearily. "We are searching them all back as far as we can."

"With great care, I hope."

"The need to be quiet slows us down," Karl replied.

"Better at a slow pace than no pace at all," Jake said. "You have found no tunnel?"

"It is hard to say. Very hard. Every opening may be the correct one, especially if what you say is true — that there would be a door or barrier before the entrance."

"There must have been," Jake confirmed. "It was a closely guarded secret, so the tunnel would have been carefully sealed."

"Then I suppose that in front of each possible entry, we have to clean away the rubble as far back as we can," Karl said. Dust caked his clothes, his hands, his face, and frosted his hair. His trio of friends appeared more than content to sit and rest and let Karl make the effort to speak. "So many bombs fell in that area that shell holes are dug into shell holes. Sometimes we cannot see where the house stood, much less where there might have been a cellar. Or tunnel. All around the bank, there are piles of rubble higher than the remains of the bank itself."

"An impossible task," Jake said, momentarily defeated.

"A difficult one," Karl contradicted. "We have three possibilities. Good ones. Narrow stairs leading down to blocked passages. We are searching for ways through."

Jake decided it was time for a visit to the frontline troops. "Corporal, can you get some rations and water up here without anyone seeing?"

"No problem, sir."

"After that, find Sergeant Morrows. Have him fill five knapsacks with provisions."

"Five, sir?"

"Five. And three canteens per man." Jake turned to Karl and continued in German, "This man will bring you something to eat. Please wait here while I see someone."

"Any reason for a rest is welcome," Karl replied, and stretched out his legs.

When Jake told Pierre his plan, Servais was not enthusiastic. "You're not going up there to boost their morale," Pierre argued. "You're going because you think maybe you can find something they can't. Which is ludicrous."

Jake finished putting on his battle dress and pulled on well-worn boots. "The kids think they might have found the entrance. I need to check it out."

"You mean you want to be there for the kill."

"I need to see it for myself before calling out the troops."

"But to go out there alone is absurd," Servais continued anxiously.

"One man can probably slip through unseen," Jake replied. "Any more would just increase our chances of being detected."

"So what do I tell Sally?"

"Nothing," Jake said, with genuine alarm. "I should be in and out within a couple of hours."

"And if not?"

Jake opened the door and checked to make sure the coast was clear. "If I'm not back by midnight, you have my express permission to call in the cavalry."

His first thought upon seeing the dark set of stairs leading down into the gloom was, this is it. His second, upon reaching the bottom stair and being confronted by several tons of bombed-out rubble was, this is impossible.

But Karl was already scrambling through a miniature hole formed high in the dusty scree. Jake watched him disappear. He called to him, "Where is your gang?"

"Opening passages elsewhere," Karl replied. "There is an iron bar across the way here. We couldn't shift it. Watch your head."

Reluctantly Jake accepted the filthy dampened rag offered by one of Karl's companions. He tied it tightly across his nose and mouth and scrambled up and into the constricting blackness.

It wasn't easy, for the opening had been made by boys much smaller than he. As Jake inched forward, the light disappeared behind him. At times his shoulders jammed; it was only by sliding one arm down and lifting the other one up that he could make it through. The second time this happened, Jake was confronted by an iron bar slicing the tunnel neatly in half, and he almost gave up in defeat. Then he realized that going backward was impossible. He grasped the rod with panic strength, and wrenched himself up and around.

To his immense relief, the hole opened up on the other side, and Jake half-slid, half-dropped into an enclosure made from the remaining portion of a basement. Supporting himself on a fallen beam, Jake rose as far as the bowed ceiling would permit.

Karl turned and inspected him in the meager light from their single flashlight. "Where is your scarf?" he asked.

"I lost it in the tunnel," Jake admitted.

With a look that relegated him to the beginners' ranks, Karl came forward, tore off a segment of Jake's shirt and doused it in water from his canteen. He handed it over, saying, "If you don't keep this on you'll be coughing your lungs up in an hour."

Once Jake was fitted out again, Karl motioned him toward a narrow opening in the far corner. "We found this hidden behind a door."

Jake took the light and followed him. Entering the enclosure, his feet scrunched on a sheet of broken glass. The chamber was very narrow and lined on both sides by floor-to-ceiling cubbyholes. Jake looked around in confusion. He then spotted palm-size labels and corks amid the rubble, and understood.

"It's a wine cellar," he called back.

"A what?"

"Rich people sometimes have cellar rooms for wine," he replied. "The wine keeps best in coolness and dark."

Jake used the flashlight to search behind the shelves, finding nothing but solid concrete. The same was true for the back wall. He returned to the main room and announced, "Nothing there."

Karl had clearly seen many such dead ends that day. He contained his disappointment well. "The next one is not so difficult to reach."

"I'm glad to hear it," Jake said, and steeled himself for the return trip.

Once out, they took a moment to replenish themselves with deep breaths of the chilly night air. Then they were up and loping forward in a crouched run, passing within three dozen paces of the stockade's lighted back entrance.

Up ahead loomed a building whose four exterior walls were almost completely intact, though nothing but a waste heap stood within. Once they were safely inside the shadows, Karl said, "My friends will help you check this out. I will go on ahead to see if they are ready for us at the next one."

Jake glanced downward. A crater had been blown through the building's foundations. "You don't think it is here?"

"The same chance here as anywhere else," Karl replied wearily. "If there is a hidden switch to spring the wall back, we cannot find it."

"Why don't you call it off for the night," Jake suggested. "You can start again tomorrow."

"Because it is twice as difficult to move about in daylight," Karl replied. "We will rest at sunrise."

Jake watched him move off, then followed the three boys into the depths of what had once been a spacious basement. When he saw where they had led him, his heart began to race again. Set in the corner facing toward the stockade was a second set of narrower stairs descending yet farther still. They ended in a dust heap, as the basement overhead had shifted slightly and sent a crumbling load down to mask whatever had stood behind. Jake saw how the gang had painstakingly cleared away enough of the bricks and refuse to expose what appeared to be a door. But there was no handle, at least not that Jake could see.

Nor were there any hinges.

As swiftly as the darkness and the need for stealth would allow, he searched the high reaches for a catch or switch that might swing the door open. He then joined the other three at the top of the stairs, searching through what remained of the central basement for something that might trigger the opening of the door.

Nothing.

Jake paused to wipe the sweat that had gathered despite the night's growing cold, and wished he could risk knocking on the door with something. He wanted to hear whether there was an echo beyond. He sighed as he realized it was impossible, and went back down the stairs to probe once more.

A scraping sound signaled what Jake thought was Karl returning. Jake mounted the stairs. It was time to tell Karl that unless one of the other entrances yielded something, he was coming back here tomorrow with a chisel.

But two steps from the top, a blow to his head sent him sprawling.

"Well, well, well," drawled an all-too familiar voice. "Lookit what we caught."

"I told you I heard somebody messing around back here." Jake instantly recognized the voice as the MP called Jenkins. "I told you these weren't no rats, Sarge."

"So give yourself a gold star and shaddap," the sergeant rapped out. "Did you get them all?"

"All three," another voice replied.

"Bring them along," the sergeant ordered. "And keep a tight grip. Those kids are slippery as eels."

"Yessir."

"I think the captain's coming around," Jenkins reported.

"Not for long he ain't." A pair of boots scraped closer, and suddenly darkness descended on Jake with a thunderbolt of pain.

Chapter Twenty-two

Jake awoke to find himself suspended from the ceiling.

The rope tied to his wrists and flung over an overhead beam had been measured out carefully. His toes barely scraped the earth, but could not bear any of his weight. As he returned to full consciousness, he realized it was not just his head that was pounding. His arms burned from being stretched out of their sockets.

"Looks like the captain's about ready to join us again, sir."

"Give him another bucketful, Jenks," the sergeant ordered. "I want him all the way round for this."

A torrent of ice-cold water slapped Jake square in the face. He coughed, spluttered, and opened his eyes.

"There you are, Burnes," the sergeant sneered. " 'Scuse me for not saluting and all."

Jake licked his lips at the taste of water, then whispered, "I thought we were supposed to be on the same side."

"Yeah, I heard that too somewhere along the

line. Guess all that went out the window when you started playing for the Germans."

"They were prisoners," Jake croaked. As his consciousness returned, fear gripped him. "They needed help."

"They were enemy, Burnes," the sergeant snarled. "Them and those kids you're always messing with."

The beast of fear filled the room, dominating Jake's universe. It was not like the fear of a coming battle. It was the terror of helplessness. Suddenly Jake's own life had been stripped from his control. There was no one to attack. There was no power to draw on for defense. The beast slithered its hands around Jake's entrails and squeezed with the awesome power of limitless dread.

Then the beast spoke with the sergeant's voice, "You can't imagine how much I've looked forward to this day, Burnes."

From the deepest reaches of his pounding heart came the silent cry, *help me.* Two words were all his mind could form.

"Now the first question is, what'd you do with the Kraut and his hoard? The second question is, what were you doing digging around here in the middle of the night?" The sergeant hefted his baton and gently pushed Jake in the chest, making him swing back and forth. "I'm gonna get the information outta you sooner or later. Just do me a favor and make it later, okay?"

Then it happened.

In a single wave that had no beginning and

no end, Jake was enveloped in peace. Before and beyond his pain, Jake saw the room reduced to human proportions. The sergeant shriveled to an anger-filled puppet. The beast was vanquished. Jake knew that beyond the slightest doubt. Come what may, he was not alone.

The sergeant was watching closely, looking for the fear he expected his words to produce. When he did not find what he sought, he growled, "You don't think I'm bluffing, do you, Burnes?"

In a split second of piercing reality, Jake was granted a gift of sight beyond the coming pain. It was not a vision of the eyes, but rather of the heart.

"What, you think your little kids are gonna come running back, storm the place, and rescue you?" The sergeant sneered. "Think again, Burnes. We've got them all locked up." He gave a slow, measured nod. His eyes never ceased their probing search. "Yeah. Ain't much chance of your little buddies breaking out and coming to the rescue. Not this time. You're mine, Burnes. All mine."

Jake saw how the beast had come to feed upon his fear, and how the Invisible had now come to *give*. Giving was His very nature. Giving in creation, in love, in comfort, in peace. Even now. Even here. No matter what they might do to his body, Jake knew in that instant of overwhelming reality that the peace was his. Forever.

"Sarge," Jenkins called from the front hallway. "You gotta get out here."

"Later, Jenks."

"Now, Sarge. Right now!"

He flung the baton across the room and stormed out. Jake heard him snort, "You're next, Jenks."

"Just take a look out there, Sarge."

There was a long moment of silence, then, "Who —"

"The whole blasted city, by the looks of things, that's who." Jenkins was beginning to panic. "There must be a coupla thousand people, Sarge. More!"

"There's another group out back," another soldier called from farther away, his voice high with tension. "And more showing up all the time."

"They've all got candles," somebody else called. "Thousands of candles."

"Do we shoot?" called a frightened voice.

"Shoot? Are you crazy? Hold your fire, everybody!" Then out the window the sergeant shouted, "This is an unlawful gathering! You people disperse or else! Go home!"

"You are holding an innocent man in there," a woman's voice called back. Her English was precise, though she had a heavy German accent. "Release him and we will go home."

"I'm warning you," the sergeant bellowed. "Disperse or else!"

"We have had enough of such warnings," the woman called back. "Years and years of warnings and terror and screams in the night. Is that why you defeated the Nazis, so you could take their place?"

"Go home!" the sergeant shouted.

The quiet murmur grew in volume.

"What's going on?" the sergeant shouted.

"Are they gonna attack?" someone yelled back.

"Do we shoot?"

"Hold your fire!" the sergeant shrilled. "These are unarmed civilians!"

"Trucks, Sarge!" called a voice. "I hear trucks!"

Then Jake did too, and he moaned with relief.

A moment later the street outside was filled with the welcome sound of grinding motors. Then a blessedly familiar voice called out, "This is Captain Pierre Servais, liaison adjutant to the Badenburg garrison. I am acting on behalf of Colonel Beecham, commanding officer. You have Captain Jake Burnes in there. I am coming in to collect him."

"He's under arrest," the sergeant screamed back.

"I am coming in to collect him," Pierre repeated. "Along with fifty fully armed men. I suggest that you avoid a major incident and release him voluntarily."

There was a spell of heavy breathing in the other room, then, "Cut him down."

"Sarge —"

"Do it!"

The rope was released. Jake's legs crumpled under him and he slumped to the floor. He tried to catch his weight with his hands, and gasped at the shock. Then he cried out again as the blood started flowing back into his limbs.

Comforting arms were soon there to support

247

him. "Take it easy, Jake." Servais and Sergeant Morrows lifted him in a double-arm sling. "Can you walk?"

"Maybe."

They made their stumbling way into the front room. A phalanx of men were still pouring in from the entrance and fanning out throughout the stockade.

"Hold it a minute," Jake ordered in a commanding yet weak voice. He nodded his head toward the MP sergeant and said to Morrows, "Let all but that man go."

"But, sir —"

Jake raised his voice as much as he could, and called out, "All who will leave peacefully are free to go, with the understanding that if any of you ever enter this city again you will be arrested on sight."

Morrows tried again. "Sir, I don't think —"

"Pass the message along," Jake cut in. "Take down the names of every man here. They're going to be shipped out by the next possible transport."

"Yessir."

"See they are loaded up and escorted out of town. Remind them there are a thousand witnesses outside ready to testify."

"More," Pierre offered.

Jake turned and looked at the sergeant for the first time since he had been cut down. He discovered that he felt no anger. "Morrows, place this man under arrest for Conduct Unbecoming."

"Try kidnapping and striking a superior officer," Pierre corrected. "Among other things."

The clarity of vision remained vivid, isolating Jake from the hatred in the sergeant's gaze. Jake saw a man shackled by his own rage, a mouthpiece for the beast. "I meant what I said," Jake replied. "All I want is a charge strong enough for him to receive a dishonorable discharge."

"Jake, listen to reason," Pierre insisted.

"What, you want my gratitude? You want me to grovel in the dirt and beg for mercy?" The sergeant snarled. "You're nothing, Burnes. And you never will be."

Jake was certain that all this man wanted, whether he knew it or not, was to provoke Jake into being like him. That was the purpose of the beast, to consume a person with rage and the desire for revenge. Then whatever happened, the outcome was sure. The beast would have conquered once more. Jake said quietly, "Morrows, I just gave you an order."

"Yessir. Consider it done, sir."

"Okay," Jake said. "Let's go."

As they moved for the door, Pierre asked quietly, "Are you sure you want to let them go like that?"

Jake struggled to put one foot in front of the other. "I'm sure."

He stepped through the entrance, and stopped once more.

Against the backdrop of a night untouched by city lights burned a sea of candles. Little flickerings of hope in an ocean of darkness. Jake's appearance was greeted by a rustling sigh, a sound as quiet and pleasant as the wind. He willed himself to stand erect, and proceeded down the stairs as best he could.

Frau Friedrichs, the woman whose son he had first taken into the clinic was there to greet him. "I could not find your treasure," she said in her heavily accented English. "But there were other ways to help."

Jake nodded. "I cannot thank you enough."

She smiled, an effort which creased her face in unaccustomed lines. "So now we both share the same difficulty, how to repay what has no price."

He looked out at the surrounding faces and asked the woman, "How did you bring all these people together so fast?"

"I did not," she replied. "You did. You see, Captain, you have many friends."

Jake spotted Karl standing beside the closest jeep, and agreed, "Good friends."

"Come on, Jake," Pierre said. "We need to get you back to HQ."

As they passed Karl, Jake said, "I owe you much."

"A life, perhaps?" Karl asked, with a smile in his voice.

Jake nodded. "A life."

"It is good to settle debts," Karl said. "I shall report to you tomorrow, Captain."

"Not early," Jake said, and allowed himself to be bundled into the jeep.

Chapter Twenty-three

The first words Jake heard upon awakening were, "I hope you are thoroughly ashamed of yourself, soldier."

Jake shifted his aching head, licked at a gummy mouth, and managed, "Water."

A hand far gentler than the voice slid in behind his neck and raised him up, while another brought the cup up to his mouth. Jake gulped greedily.

"Easy, soldier. There's no hurry."

He drank, sighed a deep sigh, and drank again. "Thank you."

The hand helped him to settle back, but did not pull away. Not yet. "Going into town all alone like that. I ought to shoot you myself."

"It had to be done," Jake whispered.

"So you say."

"I couldn't take an entire squad, looking for a tunnel that we weren't sure was even there." Jake cracked open one eye. "Is that coffee I smell?"

"I don't know if you deserve it," Sally replied, reaching for the thermos. She poured a cup and said, "Can you manage?"

"I think so." He pulled himself up, groaning at the thundering protest in his skull. Jake reached to the back of his head and felt a bandage. "What's this?"

"Six stitches," she replied. And with that the brave facade slipped away. "Oh, Jake," she whispered. "How could you?"

The sight of her quivering lip gave him the strength to push his feet to the floor. He reached over, grasped her arms, and drew her onto the bed beside him. He cradled her in his embrace, felt her trembling form, and closed his eyes to the sheer joy of nearness.

"When Pierre told me what you had done," she said, "I could have shot him, too."

"It's over, Sally," he whispered, kissing her hair.

"This time," she replied quietly.

He nodded. She was right. Now he said what he knew he had to say, what he had been thinking of on the drive into town the night before. "This is who I am, Sally. Risks are a part of my life."

The stark genuineness of his declaration brought her back far enough to look into his face. Jake went on. "I live on the edge. I guess I always will. I need you, Sally. I want you with me. But I can't change who I am just to allay your fears."

"Take it or leave it," she said bitterly.

"No," he replied, searching for words through the pounding in his head. "I will always take greater care if I know you are there waiting for me. Always. It gives me a reason to come home.

The best reason a man could ever ask for."

She sighed and found her way back to his shoulder. "What on earth am I going to do with you?"

"Love me," he whispered, holding her close. "Please."

They sat like that for a time, until Sally forced herself apart once again. "They're all waiting for you."

"Who?"

"Pierre, Morrows, half the division that's not on duty, Harry Weaver, the kids, Buddy Fox — he's still here in the infirmary, by the way. Shall I go on?"

Jake dragged himself painfully to his feet. When Sally started to stand up to help him he said, "No, I'm all right, thanks. Do you think you could find me a couple of aspirin?"

"Of course."

"Give me a few minutes to collect myself. Then I'll see Harry, okay?"

She nodded. "I'll think about what you've said, Jake."

He managed a smile. "A man can't ask for more than that."

When Dr. Weaver had finished poking and prodding and pronounced Jake as fit as any man could hope to be after what he had been through, Burnes walked down the hall and into Chaplain Fox's room. "What are you still doing in bed?"

"My ribs gave me more bother than Harry or I expected. He wanted to keep me still for another day. How are you, Jake?"

"Now that I no longer feel my head's about to come off in my hands, I'm all right."

"Pull up a chair and sit down. Sally told me what happened. You took an awful risk."

"Yeah, I guess I did." Jake eased himself down. "Something happened back there in the room when they had me tied up."

"It shows," Chaplain Fox replied.

"It does?"

"Sally noticed it too. She came down to talk with me while you were being examined. She says that when she looks at you now she notices something deeper." The chaplain gazed at him. "I agree. Do you want to tell me about it?"

Jake struggled for a moment. "I'm not sure I can," he said.

Chaplain Fox nodded. "Words can be so constricting sometimes. So incomplete. They are made for the things of this world. But sometimes our greatest revelations do not belong to this realm at all. We are given a taste of the beyond, where words do not exist."

"That's how it feels," Jake agreed. "Exactly."

"I'm glad for you, Jake," the chaplain said. "Very glad. But I want you to remember something. A life of faith is not based upon the moments of glory. Fireworks are splendid, but they soon fade. What is important is making steady, daily progress toward a life lived in Him, for Him. Do you understand?"

"I think so," Jake replied, thinking that maybe

he really did. For the very first time.

"No man can keep up the walk alone through life. All of us need the impetus and the guiding light of faith in Jesus Christ to help us stay upon the Way." Chaplain Fox bestowed upon Jake his gentle smile. "Now go out there and face the world, and know that He will be there with you."

The morning sun was brilliantly clear, and strong enough to transform the icy winterland into a vista of dripping, dancing rivulets. Jake walked slowly, exchanged salutes with grinning soldiers, took in the day with the wonder of a newborn. When he came into view of the front gate, the corporal of the guard came rushing over to greet him. "Sure is good to see you up and about, sir."

"Thank you, Corporal." Jake waved toward where Karl and his friends stood waiting beyond the gate. "It's great to be here."

The corporal pointed in Karl's direction. "They've been hanging around all morning, sir. Sally — I mean Miss Anders, sir. She came out a while ago and said you were okay and got them something to eat."

"Thank you, Corporal." Jake limped over and asked Karl, "What have you found?"

"Nothing," Karl replied. "How are you feeling?"

"Sore," he admitted. "Nothing at all?"

"Now that we can move without worry," Karl said, "it is much easier. But no more fruitful.

The best two chances we had were bombed shut. Permanently."

"The door at the bottom of the second basement staircase?" Jake asked.

"That was one of the two," Karl confirmed. "The street was hit just down from there. Whatever was beyond the door is now no more."

"At least I don't have to go down there again," Jake said.

"What do we do now?"

Jake had already decided upon that. "Keep looking. I'll meet you there in an hour or so."

"And if we find nothing?"

"If at first you don't succeed," Jake said, turning back to the gate, "then it's time to call up the heavy artillery."

Chapter Twenty-four

Jake's walk from the gatehouse to headquarters was interrupted numerous times by smiles and salutes and queries about his health. Everyone who had taken part in the raid on the stockade now felt they had a stake in his well-being.

The HQ central hall was filled to overflowing with staffers. Pierre, Sally, and Sergeant Morrows stood in front, taking charge of Jake's welcoming committee. Jake endured the attention as long as he could, but felt his patience ebb with his strength.

Finally he could stand it no more. "What is this, a holiday camp? We've got a garrison to run. Back to work!"

They responded with grins and a slow but steady withdrawal. Jake watched them go, then asked Sally, "Why is it when the colonel gives an order people jump, and when I do they grin?"

"If it had been the colonel talking under these same circumstances," Sally replied, "they would have reacted exactly the same way."

"For a moment there, I thought I was hearing the colonel," Pierre said.

"Me too," Morrows agreed, heading for the door. "Good to have you back, sir."

"Just a moment, Sergeant." Jake put a hand on his shoulder and drew him back. "Who's the best demolitions man on our silent squad?"

"The silent squad." Morrows' grin broadened. "I like that."

Jake shot him a narrow-eyed look.

Morrows straightened. "Oh, that'd be Parker, sir."

"Can he be cautious?"

"Pop a lid off a can of soup and not spill a drop, sir."

"Right. Have somebody round him up, tell him to get all he needs for a job. Then come back and join us in my office." He stopped, corrected himself, said, "I mean, the colonel's office."

"Right, sir. How large a job did you have in mind?"

"About the size of the stockade," Jake replied.

After the planning meeting was over, Jake rose from the desk. He was surprised when everyone else rose with him. "That's it, then," he said. "If we send for the trucks, it means we've struck gold. Everything goes into action then."

There were solemn nods and excited glances about the room. Jake thought to himself, time to fish or cut bait. The point of no return was about to be crossed. "Good luck, everyone. Dismissed."

As they filed out, Pierre approached him. "Are

you sure you feel like going through with this today?"

"No," Jake admitted. "But we don't know if Connors is still looking, and if so, how much time we've got left."

"Or if he's found something already," Sally agreed, joining them by the desk. "If he has, or when he does, there will be no stopping him or General Slade."

Jake looked askance at her. "What happened to all your care and concern for my well-being?"

"You look pretty fit to me, soldier," she said.

Jake sighed in mock resignation. "Are you sure you know what to do?"

"If you say that one more time I will scream," she replied. "Five minutes after we get your signal, you'll have trucks and men flooding your area."

"They'll be ready and waiting for your word," Morrows agreed from his place by the door. "Good idea you had, sir, splitting up the contingents like that. Keeps them from moving unless there's a green light."

"Can't a man have a private conversation around here?" Jake snapped.

"Just going, sir," Morrows said, not moving. "I only wanted to say I wished I was heading out with the first group."

"I understand your concern, Sergeant," Jake replied. "But I need you here to muster the troops. Now move out." When Morrows had vanished, Jake said to Sally, "Don't forget the documents and supplies. And keep trying to find Colonel Beecham. If you do —"

"You go tend to your knitting, soldier," Sally retorted. "And let me tend to mine."

Jake nodded acceptance, then glanced at the lone figure still lingering in the doorway. Pierre rubbed his nose briskly and said, "Perhaps I should go make sure the lookouts along the roads into town are in place."

"Perhaps so," Jake agreed. When he and Sally were alone, Jake asked, "That's all the send-off you're going to give me?"

She looked long into his eyes and said quietly, "I'm a lot better at hellos than goodbyes, soldier. If you expect me to get used to your risk-taking, this is one little habit you're going to have to learn to live with."

"I hope you give me the chance," he replied.

"Come back to me," she replied, "and we'll see."

Jake arrived at the stockade sweaty and clammy; coming back to the place of his ordeal hit him harder than expected. As he was posting guards, a crowd of Germans gathered. They approached, asked of his health, showed him quiet respect. One old veteran from an ancient war even threw him a rusty salute. Jake responded with smiles and a few words, and found himself settling, centering, drawing from them the strength he needed.

By the time Karl appeared he was feeling ready.

"Where have you been?"

"Checking up on one last possibility," the dusty, grime-streaked boy replied. "It's no good."

"Then round up your gang," Jake said, "and have them circulate among these people. None of my guards speak German. Tell them all we're going to be using dynamite, and that they should stand well clear."

Over the next quarter of an hour, Jake watched and waited as Parker and his two assistants wired the brig for demolition, and Karl's gang completed their passage through the throng. The crowd, however, did not disperse. As word circulated of what was about to happen, the gathering took on a carnival-like atmosphere. The crowd pointed and chattered and waved whenever Jake happened to look their way.

When Pierre joined him, Jake gestured toward the throng and asked, "Do you have any idea what this is all about?"

"You're the one who speaks their language," Pierre replied. "But I suspect they don't like Connors' men any more than you do."

"So?"

"Perhaps they think you are getting rid of the bad guys once and for all."

Jake mulled that over. "Don't contradict them."

"I wouldn't dream of it even if I could," Pierre assured him.

"And when you return to base, see if you can get word back to Connors that this is why we've blown up the building."

"That, my friend, is a grand idea. Consider it done."

Parker came hustling over. "Sorry it's taken so long, sir. See, the problem was, we've got this massive vault sitting right on top of where the second vault is supposed to be. So I had to figure out some way to blow a hole through to the bottom vault without shifting the support and sending the whole caboodle down."

"And you've done it?"

Parker grinned through the grit encrusting his face. "Sure hope so, sir."

"All right." Jake turned and surveyed the crowd of civilians. "Karl hasn't had much luck shifting them."

"They'll listen to you, Jake," Pierre said, pointing to the nearest jeep. "Stand up there where they can see you."

Jake did as he was told. Once he came into view, he raised his hands for silence and said in German, "I owe every one of you who was here last night a debt of thanks."

"Friendship is built upon mutual debts, Captain," called a stranger's voice.

"You are all friends," he agreed. "And I don't have so many friends that I can afford to lose any. So while we rid this city of a certain blight, I ask you please to disperse. And if you will not disperse, please go behind the next screen of buildings."

When the crowd had scattered, Jake turned

around. "All right, Parker. Let's blow this sucker to the moon."

"It'll be a pleasure, sir," he said, and shouted, "Take cover!"

When the warning had reached the entire periphery, Parker attached the second wire to his trigger, checked the grounds once more for strays, ducked behind the jeep where Jake and Pierre were crouched, and pushed the plunger home.

The explosion rocked the site. Debris rained down for a full thirty seconds.

As Jake picked himself up, he said to Parker, "For your sake, I hope you didn't overdo things, soldier."

Parker answered with his customary grin. "So do I, sir."

"Let's take a look."

Lazy wafts of dust drifted in the unaccustomed warmth of a sunny, windless day. Jake carefully crept forward, up the front stairway, and to the other side of what remained of the entrance. A hole had been blasted neatly through the former floor of the front hall. It gaped black and gloomy at Jake's feet.

"I set the blasts for two holes, front and back," Parker said. "In case one didn't strike pay dirt."

"Let's see what you've uncovered," Jake said, his voice tight with excitement. "Somebody get me a rope and a light."

Pierre was at his elbow. "Don't you think someone else should go down first and check things out? Like me, for instance."

263

"Not a chance." Jake wheeled around, ordered, "Secure that line to the axle of a jeep."

"You've had a hard night," Pierre pointed out. "I, on the other hand, slept like a baby."

"Rank has its privileges," Jake replied. He accepted the rope and the light, and called out, "Stand back and give me room."

Jake scrambled down the steep ledge into the cellar vault, and dropped the line through the gaping hole blown in the floor. He slithered down hand over hand, ignoring the pounding in his head. Dust clung to his face and filled his nostrils. When he felt solid ground beneath his feet, he reached for the portable lamp and switched it on. In the instant that followed, his discomfort was utterly forgotten.

Jake had landed in the central hall of a chamber that stretched the entire length of the former bank. It was sectioned into concrete-walled compartments with stout mesh doors. Each portal bore a neatly printed placket stating a name and a series of numbers. Jake walked toward the nearest door and shone his light through the mesh. He trained the beam back and forth across the compartment and saw row after row of floor-to-ceiling shelves.

The shelves were filled with treasure.

Paintings were stacked like files against the back wall. Gold and silver baubles dripped and hung like ornamental spider webs from overcrowded ledges. There were so many objects so tightly packed together that Jake could not discern all that was there. The wealth of empires and the legacies of centuries were crammed in like innumerable trinkets at a costume jewelry emporium.

"Jake? Are you all right?"

Reluctantly Jake turned his eyes from the sight. He walked over to stand beneath the hole. He looked up and said to Pierre, "Go for the trucks."

Pierre hesitated. "You are certain?"

"This is it," Jake replied. "Hurry."

Chapter Twenty-five

By the time Pierre returned with the convoy, Jake and his men had erected a series of tents; they extended in two unbroken lines from either hole to the front and back streets. Once the lines were set in place, men worked in utter secrecy, passing the treasure from hand to hand to waiting trucks. As soon as one truck was full, it moved forward to be enclosed by guards, and another empty one took its place.

Jake supervised one line of heaving, sweating men; Pierre the other. Morrows acted as a roving spotter, keeping an eye on everything, making sure that no one became greedy, watching out for anything unexpected. The trapped air within the enclosures was soon smelly and stifling, but the men did not slow down. Even when Jake ordered a halt or change of shift, they left their work with reluctance. The same air of electric urgency held them all.

Jake was on his second break, sipping a cup of soup prepared by the field kitchen, when Morrows caught his eye and motioned him over to the other side of the building.

Once Jake was out of sight of the others, Morrows said quietly, "Get a load of these, sir."

Jake stooped down. Five thick leather sacks the size of basketballs were gathered at Morrows' feet. "What have we got here?"

Morrows bent and loosened the thong holding the neck of one sack. He thrust one hand in, and came out with a fistful of gold and silver coins. "All five are just the same, sir."

Jake stared at the wealth for a split second, then came to what he would later recall as his first command decision. "Sergeant, these sacks do not exist."

"Sir?" Morrows asked, then snapped to with the light of understanding. "Right, sir. Figments of my imagination."

"Exactly. Stay here." Jake rose up, walked to the far corner. He beckoned to Karl, who lay sprawled in exhaustion with several of his gang. Even after a full night and a morning of searching for passageways, they had insisted on helping with the loading. At that point, Jake could not have refused him anything.

When Karl joined Jake and Morrows out of sight of the others, Jake pointed to one sack. "This is yours if you like. Coins will be easier to use in these times than treasure," he said. "But it's your choice."

"It is much wealth," Karl said, reluctant to touch it.

"Hide it carefully," Jake ordered him. "If you like, when I return, we can talk about how you might divide it up. But the decision is yours. Yours and your gang's."

When Karl was gone, Jake hefted one sack and said to Morrows, "Those other three are for you and the men."

"Sir?"

"I can't spare you, Morrows," Jake continued. "So you'll have to find someone you can trust to stow this away." Jake's voice turned very stern. "When it comes time to divvy it up, I expect it to be done with complete fairness. Can I trust you with that responsibility?"

"Of course, sir," Morrows said, looking in wonder at the sacks.

Jake motioned to the sack in his hands and said, "This is for the people out there."

"They saved your life," Morrows said, nodding his understanding.

"No. I'm worried about the children. They need all the help they can get to survive this winter. And the next one."

"I understand, sir," Morrows said, but his voice was troubled.

"What's the matter," Jake demanded impatiently. The sack was proving to be very heavy. "Even split up among all the men, that is going to come to a hefty bonus. They may also receive a share of the reward someday. But I want them to have this now. It's all we can safely spare, Sergeant. These other items would do nothing but attract attention and put everyone at risk."

"Oh, it's not that, sir," Morrows replied. A

shadow crossed his brow as he looked out beyond the barriers to the crowd watching with the patience of people with nowhere to go. Then he turned back to Jake and said, "I'll get Simpkins and Vance to handle this. And thank you, sir."

Jake nodded, then picked his way out of the building and on beyond the barriers. To his relief, he had no problem finding Frau Friedrichs. He walked up to her, trying to hide the strain of holding the sack, and said quietly, "Come with me, please."

Once they were well clear of prying eyes, Jake set the sack down, loosened the thong around its neck, and showed her what was inside. "You once told me your neighbors screamed at you because of your past," he told her. "If I entrust this to you, I want your solemn promise that it will be shared with all in need, without prejudice."

She gaped at the wealth. "This is Nazi gold? After all I have lived through, you wish to give me Nazi gold?"

Jake nodded. "Use it for the children and the people in most dire need."

She raised her head and searched his face for a long moment. "Someone should write a song to help us remember what you've done, Captain."

"I just want to help the children," Jake replied.

She bent over and retied the sack, lifted it to her shoulder, and said solemnly, "For the children. Upon my own son's life, I promise. For the children."

269

Chapter Twenty-six

A soldier banged down the tailgate of the truck and flipped back the canvas cover. "We're nearly there, sir."

Jake rolled over, struggling to unzip his sleeping bag. "What time is it?"

"Almost nine, sir."

His mind showed its customary reluctance to shift into gear. "In the morning?"

"Yessir." A steaming mug was thrust under his nose. "Captain Servais said to give you this, and to tell you that there's a refill waiting just outside."

"Thanks, soldier." Jake raised himself up to a sitting position, accepted the mug, took a sip, blinked in the bright sunlight. As the world gradually came into focus, he gave thanks once again for the beautiful weather.

They had driven all night. The road had been full of potholes, rutted and bombed-out, poorly marked and icy. But at least there had been no more snow. Jake had forced himself to remain awake through the first three checkpoints, but when their documents and stories had gone un-

270

questioned, he had given in to rising fatigue.

"If they ask," Jake had told Servais, "we are transporting a specially sealed shipment for General Clark in Frankfurt. No one else may touch it. Any problems have to be referred to the general personally. Nobody else."

"I heard you discussing all this with Sally before she prepared the documents," Pierre reminded him. "I have also heard you give the same story at three different checkpoints. Now climb in back and get some sleep. You're dead on your feet."

Jake had awakened at the next checkpoint, heard all proceeding smoothly once more, then allowed himself to fully relax. No guard had chosen to question a convoy of this size carrying authentic documents and under the orders of General Clark himself.

Now it was morning. And they had arrived.

Jake crawled out of the truck and walked over to where Pierre stood surrounded by a group of drivers. Troops hung from the backs of their trucks or loitered alongside, heeding Jake's strict orders to keep the vehicles fully manned at all times. A kitchen detail made its slow way down the long line of trucks and jeeps, serving coffee and what passed for army oatmeal.

To his right stretched a seemingly endless high fence, beyond which rose the main Frankfurt base. It appeared less than half finished, with dirt tracks winding off across vast partially open fields to partially constructed buildings and hangars.

Jake greeted the drivers, nodding his thanks

as Pierre refilled his mug. "Where is the main gate?"

"About a mile up ahead," Pierre replied. "How do you feel?"

"Stiff, but otherwise better. Much better." He drank the coffee, surveying the long line of vehicles pulled off the road behind him, and asked, "Is everybody ready?"

The drivers chorused a firm, "Yes, sir." Jake turned to Pierre and said, "You're in the front jeep with me."

"Everything is go, Jake," Pierre assured him. "Just as you planned."

Jake tossed the dregs of his coffee aside and handed back the cup. "Let's load up and do it."

The sergeant manning the main gates was clearly taken aback when a long line of vehicles pulled up and stopped right in front of the entrance, jamming it completely. Jake and Pierre jumped from the jeep while it was still moving; Pierre stood out in the road alongside the convoy while Jake rushed over to the astonished guardsman.

The guard saluted and said, "Sir, those trucks have got to be moved back —"

Jake handed over his fistful of documents. "Captain Jake Burnes with a special consignment for General Clark."

"Consignment of what, sir?"

"Call General Clark, Sergeant," Jake replied crisply. "Tell him that the consignment he *spe-*

cifically ordered to be delivered to him *personally* — and to *no one* else — is waiting for him at the front gates. Is that clear?"

"Yessir, I guess it is, sir." He cast a nervous glance toward the idling trucks, then started for the guardhouse phone.

"Just a minute, Sergeant. Aren't you forgetting something?"

"Sir?"

"Open the gate and let me get my trucks off this public road."

"Sir, I can't do that without —"

"I don't have time for your shilly-shallying," Jake snapped. "Those documents are all you need to get my trucks behind the safety of these gates." Jake wheeled around and shouted over the sound of the revving motors, "Do you see them?"

"Not yet," Pierre called back.

That put the guard on red alert. "See who, sir?"

"But there's some smoke in the distance," Pierre yelled with exaggerated concern. "Could be them now."

"Sergeant," Jake pressed. "I have an extremely valuable shipment that I have brought clear across this country in record time. See the date at the top of the first page?"

"Yessir. Dated yesterday." The sergeant went over and scanned the horizon again.

"I need to get these trucks inside and safe *now*."

The sergeant weakened. "I'll have to call out the guard until the general gives his okay, sir."

Jake released his pent-up breath. "That'll be fine, Sergeant. Call out anybody you like. Just open the gate, please. Now."

Reluctantly the sergeant turned to his man and said, "O.K., Charlie, raise the gate."

Jake joined his hands over his head and gave Pierre a pumping action, which Servais then repeated in plain sight of the convoy. At that, a cheer rose up and down the line. The sergeant's eyebrows went up yet another notch.

"I'll have to ask you to stay here, sir," the guard insisted.

"Of course," Jake replied. "Just remember, General Clark and no one else. He is here today, I hope."

"Yessir, I checked him in myself just under an hour ago."

Jake nodded, then yelled to Pierre as he passed, "Trucks alongside the wall, jeeps next, then the men!"

"Nobody goes near the goods," Pierre shouted back, and snapped off both a grin and a precise salute.

Fifteen minutes later, Jake was still standing there. "Still no word, Sergeant?"

"Sir, I've called every place I know and left word about you and your shipment for General Clark. Are you sure there's nobody else who —"

"This shipment is to go straight into the general's hands," Jake replied grimly. "And nobody else's."

Then a voice from behind him asked, "How about mine, son?"

Jake wheeled around, sputtered, "Colonel Beecham! What the — Where have you been, sir?"

"Hunting big game," the colonel replied, a glimmer of humor in his steely gaze. "Tell you about it later. Now then. Do you think maybe you could tell me what's got you in such an all-fired rush to see the general?"

Chapter Twenty-seven

Storing the treasure and making an official hand-over took the better part of another day. By then the colonel had already left for Badenburg — called back, he said, to a desk which had been vacant far too long. Jake's men were then gathered and paraded so General Clark could thank them. Jake was mildly disappointed that the general had no personal word for him. Not the first word.

As they set off on the return to Badenburg, however, it struck him with full force that the reason for the general's silence was the coming interview with Colonel Beecham. Jake spent the journey cataloging the rules he had broken. It made a mighty impressive list.

Jake decided his homecoming was going to be rough. Very rough indeed.

The colonel insisted on hearing Jake's report in private and alone. Jake told Beecham the entire story, including what he had done with the coins, and then accepted all blame.

When Jake had finished, the colonel only asked, "What about this German ex-soldier? What's his name again?"

"Jurgen Konrad," Jake replied. "I had him released when we started off for Frankfurt. I figured he had suffered enough, sir."

"Sit down, Captain," Colonel Beecham ordered. When Jake had settled himself in his chair, the colonel went on. "You've stepped way out of line, mister."

"Yessir, I know that, sir," Jake replied, and readied himself for the worst.

"I am only going to say this once, Captain, so listen up. We are no longer at war."

"I'm not sure I understand, sir."

"We are no longer at war," the colonel repeated. "You can't get away with bending the same rules you might have bent a year ago." He inspected Jake to make sure the message had sunk home, then continued. "Still, I think I would have probably done exactly what you did."

That shocked him cold. "Sir?"

"Or I hope I would have, anyway." Beecham cocked his chair back and propped his feet on the corner of the desk. "Now I want you to consider something. The Occupying Forces need officers like you, son. There's work to be done here. Vital work. We're not just engaged in a police action. We are responsible for helping to rebuild an entire nation."

"But, sir —"

Beecham held up his hand. "Just hear me out. Then you can say anything you like. There have been a lot of eyes on you recently. Most have liked what they've seen. A lot. These last few days were what you might call a final exam."

Jake could not help but gape. "You disappeared deliberately, sir?"

"More like we took advantage of the circumstances. The general's been busy forming the group he wants left in charge of reshaping this country. Had to make sure all the treasure hounds were rounded up and sent home. Looks like we've got them all." The colonel permitted himself a satisfied smile. "Wanted to see how you handled the pressure of command, son. You did well. Very well, in fact. The general agrees."

"He does? Sir?"

Beecham nodded. "I'm due for retirement in two months. So is Colonel Daniels up at Karlsruhe. Both of us are ready to go home. We've got families waiting, and we're not suited for what's coming next. I think you are, though, and Daniels' aide, Major Hobbs, agrees. Hobbs is scheduled to take the same ship we'll be leaving on, and feels you'd be a good man to place in charge of the new consolidated Karlsruhe command."

"Sir," Jake stammered. "I don't know what to say."

"We're pushing you for a battlefield promotion. Probably the last of its kind — in this war, anyway. Going to jump you a grade, put you right in as colonel, acting officer in charge, to be confirmed in ninety days. What do you say?"

Jake was left speechless.

"It's the chance of a lifetime, if you ask me.

I'd urge you to jump on it with both feet." Beecham stood up. In a daze, Jake rose and accepted the colonel's hand. "You're a good man, Burnes, and a good officer to boot. One of the finest I've served with, and I've served with some dillies. Go think it over, and let me know what you decide."

Jake almost collided with Pierre as he left the colonel's office. Servais searched Jake's face. "It was bad, yes?"

Jake tried to collect himself. "I'm not sure."

"I don't see any blood. There are no guards. What happened?"

Jake pulled him into the hallway and told him the news.

Pierre said, "I don't understand."

"What's there to understand?"

"This is great news. Why do you look so glum?"

"I don't know whether I want to accept or not."

Pierre smiled broadly. "My friend, may all your life be filled with such troubles as this."

"This isn't a joke, Pierre."

"Wait. I too have news." Pierre drew himself up to full height. "You are now looking at the new commander of the French garrison at Baden-burg."

"You?"

"Don't look so shocked. I think they have made an excellent choice." He patted Jake on the shoulder. "This of course would mean that I shall be close enough to offer advice whenever you are at a loss, Colonel."

Jake arrived back at the main camp to find Sally Anders pacing the length of his barracks. "I've been cooling my heels around here for over an hour, soldier. Are you going to accept?"

He gazed at her. "Aren't there any secrets around here?"

"Stow it, soldier. I asked you a direct question. I think I deserve a direct answer."

Jake sank down on the bed and replied, "I don't know."

She sat down beside him. "Would it help any if I told you I was accepting a posting to Berlin?"

Jake was both surprised and pleased. Then he thought for a minute, and pointed out, "Berlin is a long away from Karlsruhe."

"It's a lot closer than Ottawa," she replied. "Which was where I was headed until about three hours ago."

"You did that? For me?"

"I bet colonels in charge of bases can find lots of reasons to go hobnobbing with the senior brass in Berlin."

"Is that what you're going for? To hobnob with the officers?"

"Maybe. At least with one in particular. That is, if he'll let me. Hobnob, I mean."

"I can't see anybody turning you away, Sally," he replied seriously.

"I'm not interested in just any old officer body," she replied crisply. "One recently promoted colonel is the one I've got my eye on."

"Oh, really?"

She nodded. "If he'll have me."

"What if he wants you to give up the big city of Berlin for a little nowhere town like Karls-ruhe?"

She took a deep breath. "Then I guess he's got his work cut out for him." She rose before he could reach for her, and said, "That's about all the risk-taking this girl can manage just now, especially with a desk piled high with transfer and promotion orders, and another soldier waiting to speak with you."

"Let him wait," he said. "Come and sit down."

"Later," she promised. She bent down and planted a solid kiss right where it belonged. Then she smiled, wiped the red smudge off his mouth, and said, "Can't have our newest colonel receiving his first official visitor wearing lipstick."

"Sally —"

"Don't, Jake. I'm shaky enough already." She bestowed upon him a trace of the tenderness he knew was there, and said in parting, "We'll have time for this later."

Jake was still staring at the door when Sergeant Morrows appeared, knocked, and asked, "Sir, could I speak with you for a moment?"

"Too much too fast," Jake muttered.

Morrows hesitated. "Sir?"

"Nothing, Sergeant," he replied. "Come on in."

"Thank you, sir."

Jake pointed to his footlocker. "I'm afraid this is the only seat I can offer you."

"Oh, no thank you, sir." Morrows remained standing, shifting his weight nervously from one foot to the other.

"What's on your mind?"

Morrows twiddled with his cap and said, "It's like this, sir. Me and the boys've been thinking."

"Always a dangerous sign."

"Yessir. Anyway, what we wanted to ask was, are you taking any share of the loot?"

Jake jerked to full-alert status. "What's that got to do with anything?"

"We'd just like to know, sir."

"I'll get a share of the reward, just like everybody else," Jake replied. "Someday. Maybe."

"That's not what I mean, sir."

"If you're talking about the coins, then the answer is no. That was intended for you men."

"That's sorta what we figured, sir. Me and the men, well . . ." Morrows hesitated.

"Go on, spit it out, man."

"We want to give it back, sir," Morrows said in a rush. "All of it."

Jake was completely dumbfounded. "Give it back?"

"The coins." The effort was costing Morrows dearly. "It's like this, sir. We got back pay coming outta our ears, at least compared to some. And with this new GI bill, we'll be getting a real leg up when we get home." He waved a hand to encompass the entire outside world. "But these folks, sir, what've they got going for them?"

"Nothing," Jake said quietly. "Absolutely nothing."

"That's what we mean." Morrows swiped at the perspiration beading his forehead. "They need it a lot worse than we do."

Jake shook his head at the enormity of what he was hearing. "I don't know what to say."

"The word's out that you might be sticking around, sir," Morrows went on. "We'd like you to keep it and use it wherever you think it'll do the most good."

Jake searched the sergeant's face. "You didn't pressure anyone to go along with this?"

"Nossir. It just sort of happened, I guess you could say. I can't explain it any better than that. But everybody agrees. All of us, sir."

"This will mean a lot to these people, Sergeant," Jake said solemnly. "It may make the difference between life and death for some. This is a very great and generous act."

Morrows shrugged and said, "We'll probably regret it like the dickens in the morning, sir."

"I doubt it," Jake replied. "I doubt it very much." He rose to his feet and offered the sergeant his hand. "For all those who will never know what you've done, accept my thanks, Sergeant. And pass it along to everyone else. Tell them . . ." Jake paused, then said simply, "I have never been prouder of anyone, at any time, than I am of all of you."

Toward dusk, Jake pulled out of the main gates and started down the road, only to find Karl walking up the road toward him. Jake stopped and turned off the jeep. "Where are your friends?"

"I wished to speak with you alone," Karl replied.

"Come aboard," Jake offered.

The boy took the seat beside him. "So it is done."

"Not entirely," Jake replied, thinking of the promotion he was about to accept.

"No," Karl agreed, misunderstanding him. Then he confessed, "I do not know what to do with our gold."

"It is a great deal of wealth," Jake agreed.

Karl slumped down even farther. "That all these riches could cause so many problems."

"There are banks with safety deposit boxes," Jake replied. "And there will be traders for the coins later when the markets are restored. And friends to offer help in the meantime."

"Banks and markets are for people with papers," Karl replied bitterly. "And friends go away to distant lands."

"Not this friend," Jake corrected him. "And papers can be arranged."

"What are you saying?"

"I happen to know for a fact," Jake answered, "that a certain commander of the Karlsruhe garrison is looking for a squad of young German men and women to help out around the base.

Orderlies for the Officers' Mess, clerical help, assistants in the PX, that sort of thing."

"Commander?" Karl gaped. "You?"

"The job pays three square meals a day and provides a wealth of experience," Jake went on. "Along with a warm bunk and pocket money. This means you can leave your funds untouched until your feet and your nation are firmly established upon solid ground. The one condition is that all jobholders must go to school."

Karl made a face. "School."

"You will thank me in the end," Jake promised. "And I will see that you all receive papers."

"You will do this? For me?"

"A life is a great debt to owe somebody," Jake replied. "I recall someone telling me that once."

Karl's face split into a mighty grin. "We were a great team."

Jake corrected him, "We still are."